J

Tournament Upstart

The Falcons began to collect the dividends on a lifetime of playing together. The impossible passes were completed because both passer and receiver knew each other's abilities, limits, and inclinations. The instinctive knowledge of what a teammate was going to do next provided screens for shooters, lanes for dribblers. Jimmy, having played with his teammates only the one season, was outside the mystical connection that was producing miracles. But his jump shots and ball handling were every bit a part of the unstoppable force of the Falcons sailing through the fourth quarter.

By the time the clock ticked into the final minute of play, the Falcons stood out front with an eleven-point lead, 44–33.

As the last minute ticked away, the roar of the crowd swept down over them like an ocean wave, *"Fal-cons! Fal-cons!"*

Tournament Upstart

Thomas J. Dygard

BEECH TREE
New York

Published by Morrow Junior Books
a division of William Morrow and Company, Inc.
1350 Avenue of the Americas, New York, NY 10019
www.williammorrow.com

Printed in the United States of America.

The Library of Congress has cataloged the Morrow Junior Books edition of *Tournament Upstart* as follows:
Dygard, Thomas J.
Tournament upstart.
Summary: Under the leadership of their new young coach, a Class B high school basketball team from the Ozark foothills challenges big-city schools for the state championship.
ISBN 0-688-02761-X
[1. Basketball—Fiction] I. Title. PZ7.D9893To 1984 [Fic] 83-25039

First Beech Tree Edition, 1998
ISBN 0-688-16369-6
10 9 8 7 6 5 4 3 2 1

For my first grandson, Tom

One

Coach Floyd Bentley stepped to the edge of the glistening basketball court and wondered for the hundreth time what he had gotten himself and his team into.

He was still wearing the plaid mackinaw jacket buttoned up to the neck against the chilly, blustery March weather outside.

Behind him, the eight members of the Cedar Grove High Falcons basketball team walked to the edge of the court. They were stretching their arms, unbending from the three-hour drive to Talbott State University in Floyd's van.

Floyd looked around at the empty seats in the arena—sixteen thousand of them—rising from the floor to the ceiling in a giant bowl. Back home in Cedar Grove, a crowd of a few hundred was considered big. At tiny Morrison State College, where Floyd played college basketball for four years, the gym was ancient and cramped, and the Morrison

1

State opponents' gyms were no better. They each could have fit in one end of this place. Floyd, gazing at the endless rows of seats, wondered how much noise sixteen thousand cheering fans made. Probably a lot.

At the age of twenty-three, Floyd looked hardly older than his players. Fresh out of college and back in his hometown of Cedar Grove, he was in his first year as coach. He was tall, standing six feet four inches, and lean. His slender frame and lifelong habit of carrying himself rigidly erect made him appear even taller. His straight black hair, neatly trimmed, was combed to one side. A couple of unruly sprigs of hair standing up in the back added to his boyish appearance. He usually wore jeans and a plaid shirt, but on this occasion he had on a pair of new navy-blue slacks and a light-blue sports shirt, also new.

From behind him Floyd heard a low whistle from one of the players. He recognized it. He had heard that whistle most of his life. It came from Eddie Bentley, his younger brother, the Falcons' center. The whistle meant Eddie was impressed. Eddie, the team's only senior starter, stood six feet six inches, two inches taller than Floyd. He was the power hub of the Falcons' basketball team.

Another player spoke softly. "Just like the places you see on television," said Gene Montgomery. Floyd could imagine the expression of awe on Gene's face. Red-haired and freckle-faced, Gene laughed and joked a lot. But at his forward position he was the steadiest player on the Falcons' team.

"Uh-huh," replied Jimmy Gunn, Gene's partner at forward. Jimmy was the only boy on the team who had not lived all his life in the tiny town of Cedar Grove. His voice sounded casual, almost bored, certainly unimpressed, as always.

Floyd did not turn to acknowledge the comments of his players.

The cleanup crews in their white coveralls were the only signs of life among the rows of seats. Dragging green trash bags, they scooped up the paper cups, popcorn boxes, and paper napkins left by the crowd at the two afternoon games. They were preparing the arena for the two coming night games.

This was Thursday, the first day of the final round of the Class A state high-school basketball tournament: four games—two in the afternoon, two at night—pitting the winners of the eight district tournaments. Then tomorrow, two games producing the two finalists to play for the championship on Saturday night.

Floyd's Cedar Grove Falcons, easy winners of their district tournament, had drawn the first of the night games, and the toughest of opponents: the Warren Tech Trojans, defending champions, only twice beaten in the regular season and heavy favorites to win the crown again.

Floyd had not counted on drawing Warren Tech as the opponent in the first game. But there was a lot lately that Floyd had not counted on.

Two weeks ago, when his Falcons finished their regular season with a 26–4 record and a sixteen-game

3

winning streak, the idea of stepping up from the Class B ranks and entering the Class A tournament against the big schools seemed natural enough, even logical and exciting.

Cedar Grove High, with its enrollment of just under two hundred, located in a village in the Ozark foothills north of Little Rock, was rated Class B with all the other tiny schools in the state. Properly, the Falcons belonged in the Class B tournament. But the rules of the Arkansas Athletic Association allowed a Class B team, if it chose, to enter the Class A tournament, beginning with the district playoffs.

The Class A crown was the *real* one. The Class B crown was, well, Class B.

Nobody knew who had first suggested aloud that the Falcons should step up from their class and shoot for the Class A crown. Some said Floyd had first voiced the idea. Although he admitted to having the thought cross his mind, he had heard it first in the form of a question from a teacher at Cedar Grove High: "Are you going to try for the Class A championship?" Others said the players, riding on top of the world after their strong finish in the regular season, had started the chatter. Or maybe it was the exuberant fans of Cedar Grove. Nobody knew for sure.

Either way, it suddenly seemed that everyone—at the soda fountain in Mr. Phipps's pharmacy, in the checkout line at the Johnny Reb Supermarket, at the car wash, on the street corners, in the corridors at Cedar Grove High—was talking up the idea.

After all, the Falcons had whipped some Class A

4

teams in their part of the state on the way to building their 26–4 record. Why not knock off a few more of the big schools and bring home the big trophy?

Posters with red lettering and black trim—the Cedar Grove school colors—appeared in the windows at the pharmacy and at the supermarket: CLASS A—ALL THE WAY. Out of nowhere, banners of red and black proclaimed the same slogan in the corridors of Cedar Grove High's ancient red-brick building.

When Floyd had put the question to a vote of the players in the dressing room after practice one afternoon, the result had been a loud whoop and a cheer—and no dissenting votes.

"We'll whip the city slickers," Gene Montgomery had shouted with a laugh, and everyone had cheered.

The word of the formal decision had spread quickly through Cedar Grove, and the people responded with whoops and cheers of their own. They had echoed Gene's statement. Everyone, Floyd and his players included, grinned at the boast. The Falcons were ready to go for—and win—the big one. They were going to be the Class A champs.

Then slowly, and at first with only the tiniest of hints, doubts began to crop up. First among the townspeople, then among the students at Cedar Grove High, and finally among the players themselves. Perhaps the Falcons' decision had been too hasty. After all, Cedar Grove High was a small school with a small squad and an inexperienced coach. The best of the big schools were more powerful, more polished than anything the Falcons had seen all season.

Maybe the Falcons should have stayed in their place, Class B. Perhaps they were good enough to win the Class B crown. That would be better than getting themselves blown off the court by a high-powered Class A team. But it was too late. The Falcons were committed.

Floyd had shrugged off the first stories he had heard coming out of the conversation around the window table at Big John's Cafe where all the businessmen gathered for their morning coffee.

"Floyd is going to take our boys up there and get them humiliated." It was Big John Raymond doing the talking. "And all of it on television, for the whole state to see," he added.

"Aw, c'mon, John, the Falcons are pretty good," someone said.

"Been playing other little teams just like ourselves, with coaches just as greenhorn as Floyd," Big John said.

"Floyd's done a pretty good job, I think," another said.

"Wait and see," Big John said.

John Raymond, a member of the Cedar Grove school board and one of the biggest property owners in the county, always was a voice to be heeded.

But Floyd figured that Big John, for all his influence, was neither a coach nor a player with the Cedar Grove Falcons. Big John did not devise the tactics, call the plays, draw up the starting lineup. Floyd did those things. Big John did not dribble or pass or shoot. The players—Eddie, Gene, Jimmy, the others—did those things. Floyd and the players had won the games, not Big John with his remarks at the window table of the cafe.

Win or lose, Floyd might have to deal with John Raymond's displeasure at contract time, but for now he had other matters on his mind. He was not worried about the talk at the window table.

Not worried, that is, until the evening that Gene Montgomery's father telephoned him at home. Wilson Montgomery ran a hardware store on the square. Floyd had worked for him one summer during high school. A former Falcons player himself, Wilson Montgomery always had been an ardent fan, dating back before Floyd's own days as a high-school player. Now, with a son in the starting lineup, he never missed a game and frequently dropped in at practice. Floyd called him the honorary assistant coach, and Wilson Montgomery did indeed help him on occasion when a second adult hand was needed. He had actually coached from the bench once when Floyd was sidelined by a heavy cold.

"Floyd, there's talk around town, and—"

"I heard that Big John thinks we're going to get ourselves humiliated."

"It's not just that."

"What is it?"

Wilson Montgomery hesitated. "Well, a lot of people are saying that you just want to take the Falcons to the Class A tournament to"—he paused, apparently finding the next words awkward—"to advertise yourself for a better job, and maybe advertise

Eddie for a scholarship at some college. They're saying you're willing to gamble the kids . . ."

Floyd no longer heard the words. He bit his lower lip. Were the charges true? Maybe. He had no doubts that a strong—or even just respectable—showing with a Class B team in the Class A tournament would cast him instantly as a young coach to watch. And, yes, he might someday want to move to a larger school. Cedar Grove, although home, hardly offered great opportunities for a coaching career. Cedar Grove coaches always were moving on to something better. That was what had left the job open for him after graduation from Morrison State College. Last year's coach had moved on to a better job. It was nothing new for Cedar Grove to be looking for a new coach. So what was so bad about the possibility of Floyd moving on? He had not discussed it with anyone, not even Eddie or Gene's father. But at the same time, he had made no promises about staying forever.

As for Eddie, it was true that exposure in the Class A tournament against the best teams in the state would give a boost to his stock. Already taller and stronger than Floyd, Eddie had the makings of a standout player at a major college. Perhaps Eddie need not settle for tiny Morrison State College, as Floyd had done. But this, too, Floyd had never discussed with Eddie.

No, Floyd was certain that neither his own nor his brother's future had been the determining factor in his support of the Falcons entering the Class A tournament and taking aim at the big crown.

8

"The players voted the move," Floyd said flatly.

"All right," Mr. Montgomery said. "I just thought you ought to know what they're saying around town."

Floyd hung up the telephone slowly, knowing full well the impact of such chatter in a small town.

The next day, while the players were dressing for practice, Floyd overheard Jimmy Gunn talking to Gene.

"You've just never seen a good—really good—team from a big—really big—school," Jimmy said.

That was all Floyd heard, but it was enough to put a frown on his face. First, the seeds of the idea that Floyd was willing to risk the humiliation of his players for the chance of personal gain. Now, the first hint among his players that humiliation was inevitable.

Jimmy Gunn was familiar with the big schools and their brand of basketball, and all of the Falcons knew it. Jimmy had transferred in at the start of this year from a large high school on the outskirts of Houston. He and his mother were living in Cedar Grove, the home of her parents, for two years while his father, an engineer, completed a road-construction project in Saudi Arabia. Jimmy, deadly with jump shots from the corner, frequently led the Falcons in scoring. But he never managed—or even tried—to fit in with the Cedar Grove boys. He wore a different kind of clothes. He talked in a different way. He wore his hair in a different, over-the-ear modish cut. He was a stranger in Cedar Grove and a stranger on the team, and he seemed determined to remain that way.

Worse yet, he made no secret about looking down on everything in Cedar Grove—the school building, the gym, the dressing room, the team's faded uniforms, even the new and inexperienced young coach. Once in mid-season, only the presence of Wilson Montgomery prevented a fight in the dressing room when Jimmy made a crack about John Hartley's "farmer clothes." Floyd was not there at the moment. When he heard about the flare-up later, he silently thanked his lucky stars that Jimmy's target had been John Hartley. John, a substitute, seldom saw action, so he and Jimmy rarely had to work as part of a team together on the court. If the target of Jimmy's jibe had been Gene or Eddie, real trouble would have developed immediately. The episode was bad enough as it was, but an open break among the starters would be sure to unravel the Falcons' teamwork.

None of it came as a surprise to Floyd. He had been warned by none other than Jimmy's father, in town briefly before taking off for Saudi Arabia.

"Jimmy didn't even want to come out for basketball," Joe Gunn had told Floyd in the gym before the second day of practice last October. "I think you ought to know that. He was heartbroken about leaving Houston. He hasn't liked what he has seen here—has refused to like it."

Floyd had nodded his understanding. He had seen the new boy—so different, so apart from the others—in the corridors of Cedar Grove High.

"Fortunately, Jimmy and I always have gotten

along well. We've fished and camped together. He listens to what I say. In this case, it took a lot of talking, but he finally agreed to play basketball, and I hope we've got him on track."

Floyd appreciated the frank talk. It prepared him for what was to come. But while Jimmy was indeed playing basketball, Floyd never had found reason to describe him as "on track."

Now Floyd wondered about the impact of Jimmy's words on Gene and the others. Maybe the Falcons were paying no attention to the warnings from the big-city boy. But maybe they were listening to him. Floyd had no way of knowing.

The Falcons' easy victory in the Class A district tournament, winning for themselves a place among the final eight in the championship round, did little to help the situation.

"No wonder the Falcons won the Class A district tournament in a breeze," Big John told his listeners around the window table. "This district has got the weakest Class A teams this year that I've ever seen."

Jimmy Gunn seemed to agree. "A bunch of patsies," he told Gene in the dressing room after the Falcons had thrashed Reedsville by a 54–39 score for the district championship. "Just wait and see what's coming."

Nobody was saying, "We'll whip the city slickers"—not the students, not the townspeople, not even the players.

But now the best of the city slickers—the winners

of the Class A district tournaments around the state—were at hand.

Floyd, standing at the sideline of the court, took one last look at the empty seats rising on all sides, trying to banish all the unpleasant pictures of the last two weeks. He turned to his players and managed a smile that he did not feel. "C'mon, we'll get something to eat," he said. "We've just got time before we get dressed."

TWO

The rumbling of the crowd filling the seats above them could be heard in the dressing room where the Falcons were changing into their game uniforms.

To Floyd, the noise had the muffled sound of distant thunder in the Ozark foothills around Cedar Grove.

Around him, the Falcons were almost dressed in their game uniforms. Gene Montgomery was tying a shoe, a half-smile on his face in anticipation of the game. Beside Gene, Jimmy sat leaning back against a locker, legs crossed and arms folded over his chest. He was staring into space. Eddie was perched on a training table, leaning forward, gazing at the floor.

Floyd glanced at the twins, Ray and Roy Barton, the Falcons' guards. Sophomores, they were the youngest players on the team. They were a hard pair to read. If they felt any emotions—excitement, nervousness, delight, fear—they kept them hidden behind blank expressions. They were pulling on their shirts. Floyd could tell them apart only by their numbers: number eleven was Roy, number twelve was Ray.

William Logan, the sixth player on the team and the Falcons' only reliable substitute, was standing next to Eddie. At six feet four inches, William would have been the Falcons' starting center if it were not for Eddie. He had been slated for a starting forward position until the sharpshooting Jimmy Gunn had appeared on the scene from Houston. Now William spent most of his time on the bench. He filled in for Eddie at center and for Jimmy and Gene at forward, but only when one of them was in foul trouble or the game was a runaway victory.

John Hartley, a senior, and Bobby Watson, a sophomore, completed the ranks for the Cedar Grove Falcons. John was too chubby, too slow, and too poor a shot to win much playing time. But he would win a letter this year. It would be his reward for four years of trying. Every time Floyd saw John approach his locker, whether to exchange his clothes for his game uniform or to dress after a game or a practice, the words *farmer clothes* came to mind. Floyd was sure the words recurred to John, too, because John and Jimmy Gunn had not spoken since the explosion eight weeks ago. Bobby Watson, a cousin to the Barton twins, was built like them—small but wiry and quick. However, he lacked the twins' coolness under pressure and their steady ball-handling abilities. Fortunately for all of them, Bobby agreed that he was not

14

the measure of his cousins, and he took his bench-riding role in good humor.

Floyd, seated on a bench, watched the players and listened absently to the sounds of the crowd above them. Somewhere among those sixteen thousand fans were the dozen or so people who had made the trip from Cedar Grove for the game. Wilson Montgomery would be weaving his way through the crowd to the dressing room any minute. He drove, and brought the four Cedar Grove cheerleaders with him in his station wagon. Floyd's own parents, there to watch one son coach and another play, were probably settling into their seats. Jimmy Gunn's mother and probably his grandparents were arriving. A smattering of other parents and friends, but not many, were carrying the red and black of the Falcons into the huge arena. And certainly missing was Big John Raymond.

Floyd recalled Wilson Montgomery's account of Big John's latest comments. "So it's Warren Tech, huh?" he had grunted when the pairings were announced. "Worse than I feared."

"Going up for the game?" someone had asked.

Big John had stared in silence at the man. The question was too dumb to dignify with an answer. No, he was not going to be driving three hours up and three hours back to witness the humiliating obliteration of the Falcons under the leadership of an uppity young coach who had taken leave of his senses.

Floyd passed a hand over his forehead, trying to wipe away these thoughts. The time had passed for worrying. Now they were going to play the Warren Tech Trojans.

The time had ended, too, for the mapping of strategy.

From the hour the pairings were announced, Floyd had spent every spare moment charting the tactics that would defeat Warren Tech. He talked on the telephone incessantly, calling coaches whose teams had played Warren Tech during the regular season. He needed to know everything—strengths, weaknesses, style of play, what to fear, what to hope for. This form of telephone scouting was standard procedure among the high-school coaches. Somebody from Warren Tech was undoubtedly making the same calls to coaches whose teams had played Cedar Grove.

Almost everything that Floyd learned about the Warren Tech Trojans qualified as bad news. The Trojans had four of their five starters back from the team that won the state championship last year. Most of the coaches rated the Trojans as stronger this year than last.

Their center was the physical equal of Eddie, standing the same six feet six inches tall, and had won a place on the all-state team in his junior year. Now a senior, he was better than ever. Eddie was in for a tough night.

The Trojans' guards were dribbling magicians and deadeye shots from the outside. The twins would have their hands full.

The forwards, both standing six feet four inches, were strong rebounders and able shooters.

Worse yet, the Trojans had depth on their squad. Behind every starter, a capable substitute sat on the bench, awaiting his chance.

Floyd had listened to his fellow coaches—people he had never met, but colleagues willing to help—and he took copious notes, trying to weave the facts into a pattern that would spell victory for his Falcons.

More than anything else, the word *depth* caused Floyd to frown. His own bench strength amounted to the single figure of William Logan. Beyond William, the depth of the Falcons offered precious little ability—the slow and inept John Hartley, and the inexperienced Bobby Watson.

In the end, Floyd knew, the outcome was going to rest with the individual skills of his starting players—Eddie's hook shots and rebounding, Jimmy's jump shots from the corner, Gene's playmaking and passing, the concentration and tenacity of the twins. And, Floyd told himself, a little bit of luck.

Gene Montgomery's father arrived. In his late thirties, with the same red hair he had given his son, he had the physique and stride of a former athlete. He was smiling, and his booming voice broke the silence of the dressing room.

"All set?" he asked. "Ready to go?"

"Hey, who is it we're playing, anyway?" Gene piped.

Somebody laughed nervously.

"We're all set," Floyd said. "Just waiting."

Gene's father said, "See you after the game. Good luck." He left, closing the door behind him.

Almost immediately somebody knocked at the dressing-room door and a voice from the corridor sang out, "Time, coach."

Floyd looked around at the players. "Let's go," he said.

The players got to their feet. Floyd opened the door, letting the roar of the crowd in upon them. The players—Gene first, then Jimmy, then the others—walked out the door into the corridor and turned left toward the court. Floyd stood at the door and watched them go, and then followed the last player, William Logan, out.

They were a serious bunch, Floyd thought as he followed them down the corridor. Too uptight? Maybe. But maybe not. Floyd knew from his own playing days, which ended only a year ago now, that a little nervousness could be a big help going into a game—it made the adrenalin flow; it helped a player move more quickly, jump higher. He wondered if a little nervousness helped a coach, too. He hoped so.

When Floyd emerged from the corridor, his players were strung out along the sideline, headed for their bench.

All around the huge bowl, every seat was occupied. Floyd had never seen so many people in one place. The arc lights bathed the scene in a brilliant white, leaving no shadows. High above the crowd on the opposite side of the arena, figures in the press box moved in silhouette. Giant scoreboards at each end of the arena listed the teams and their players in lights, with digital clocks marking the playing time remaining.

Floyd walked toward the bench behind his players.

Suddenly, a mighty roar erupted. At the same instant, as if they had been fired out of a cannon, a stream of players wearing bright green warm-up suits with silver trim burst into view, racing single file along the opposite sideline.

A whole section of fans rose as one, waving green pennants and shrieking.

The Warren Tech Trojans, defending state champions, were taking the court.

Floyd unconsciously stopped and stared at the scene.

The line of running players, followed by the head coach and the two assistant coaches, made the half circle around the end of the court and gathered in front of their bench.

Floyd glanced at his players. They, like he, were gaping at the scene.

"Let's go, let's go," Floyd called out above the cheers as he walked past William Logan, the twins, then Jimmy and Gene, heading for the bench.

Floyd heard Gene's voice as he walked by. "Pretty fancy," Gene said.

No basketball player in the history of Cedar Grove ever had a warm-up suit in the school colors.

The Falcons' uniforms—black shorts that had turned to gray, and red shirts that had turned to a flat pink, as a result of repeated washings—seemed somehow out of place in the bright lights of the giant arena alongside the glittering Warren Tech Trojans.

Floyd slowed his pace to let the players pass him on the way to the bench, then followed them. He suddenly found himself facing a man wearing a green warm-up suit with silver trim. Slender and shorter than Floyd, the man had a reddish face and a heavy shock of white hair that matched the suit's silver trim. He was smiling at Floyd and extending his right hand.

"Coach Bentley, I'm Bernie Dodge. Congratulations on being here in the final round, and best of luck."

Floyd took the extended hand and pumped. "Thanks, and the same to you."

Bernie Dodge, still smiling, turned and trotted back to his team.

The Falcons walked onto the court for their warm-up drills, and Floyd stood back watching, first his own players, then the Warren Tech Trojans. Floyd believed warm-up drills revealed a lot about the kind of game a team was going to play. He liked to see in his own team an air of concentration, a sense of precision in the movements of the players, a feeling of cohesiveness among the individuals. Staring at his Falcons, he thought he saw the signs he liked.

Turning to the other end of the court, for the first time Floyd saw the players whose names and talents he had burned into his brain for the last four days. With a frown, he had to admit that they looked every bit as good as their reputations.

Floyd delivered his lineup to the scorer's table at

the sideline between the two benches, then returned to the Falcons' bench and sat down.

He saw Jimmy let fly with a jump shot and then turn to look at the Trojans at the other end of the court. Clearly, Jimmy Gunn was on the wrong team. Coming from a big school on the outskirts of Houston, he belonged in that long line of sparkling green warm-up suits that had circled the court so majestically, not in the bunch of faded uniforms of the Cedar Grove Falcons making their lackadaisical entrance. He belonged with those players who wore the same haircut and the same confident—almost blasé—expression that he wore. Jimmy did not belong with the team that arrived in "farmer clothes." The feelings were written all over Jimmy's face, easy for Floyd to read.

Floyd shrugged off the thought and got to his feet. The players were returning to the bench for the last few seconds before the opening tip-off.

The arena was strangely quiet now. The fans from the first to the top row were seated, the only sound a low murmur of conversation. Even the large patch of green—the crowd of Warren Tech fans—was quiet and still.

Floyd, with his team around him, glanced down the sideline at the Warren Tech bench. He saw the head of white hair bobbing in the center of a crowd of players, five of them stripped of their warm-up suits, ready to play. Bernie Dodge was delivering the last words of advice before the opening tip.

Floyd leaned into the players around him, and they clasped hands in the center, all eight of them and the coach. He had only one thing to say. "Remember this," he said softly, "the hoops are no higher here than back home, and they're just as big."

He looked around at the serious faces, meeting the eyes of each player.

They pumped hands three times and broke the group.

The starters took the court: Eddie at center, Gene and Jimmy at the forward positions, the twins at guard.

Floyd turned and sat on the bench with his three substitutes. He folded his arms over his chest and crossed his legs, trying to appear relaxed and confident. He hoped nobody could see that his hands were shaking and his heart was pounding furiously.

But before the referee even spun the ball up for the opening tip-off, Floyd was leaning forward, legs spread, elbows on his knees, hands clasped together so tightly that the knuckles were white. His jaw was clenched as he stared at the scene on the court.

Three

The big Warren Tech center outjumped Eddie and flicked the ball back to a short, wiry guard with a mop of reddish hair half-covering his ears.

The guard dribbled in place a moment, allowing his teammates time to take up their positions for the first assault on the goal.

Floyd, clenching and unclenching his hands between his knees, watched the action on the court. The Trojans were a methodical team. Every play was a carefully charted exercise, not getting under way until all players were in position and ready. Then, every movement was part of a precisely choreographed plan designed to screen out defenders, lure them out of position, leave them off balance, and move the ball in for a field goal. Nothing was left to chance in their offense. Everything was planned and executed to achieve the ultimate objective of the game of basketball—putting the ball in the basket.

One of the twins, Roy, following Floyd's advice,

moved in to harass the guard with the ball. It was never too early in a play to start trying to break the pattern of the offense. The Trojans, if their pattern of offense were broken, would fall back, regroup, and begin again. And therein, Floyd figured, lay the best and brightest hope of the Falcons. Every disruption of the Trojans' offense meant more passing and ball handling, and more chances of a fumble, an interception, a steal—and a field goal for the fast-breaking Falcons racing down the court.

Roy waved his right hand in the face of the guard and stabbed at the bouncing ball with his left hand. The guard dribbled back a half step, eluding his thrust. The twin followed him.

Then, with a quickness that made Floyd blink, the guard continued the movement backward—with a dribble behind his back—and turned and raced away from Roy.

Floyd felt himself flinch, sharing Roy's humiliation. Everyone knew that the twins never showed any emotion, but this time one of them did. Roy, left flat-footed and alone on the court, turned a deeper shade of red than his faded shirt.

The green-clad crowd in the section across the court arose with a roar, a mixture of cheers for the guard's flashy play and laughter at Roy's confusion and embarrassment. Their Trojans were off to a good start, teaching the upstart team a lesson in basketball.

The guard, a cocky smile on his face, dribbled easily across the center stripe. Roy, now recovered, took off in pursuit.

The cheers died down but the tinkling sounds of the laughter lingered. Floyd thought it would never end. He knew he would hear its echoes the rest of his life. So would Roy. Floyd wanted to call the boy off the court and tell him that it didn't matter. Maybe if he cupped his hands over Roy's ears, Roy would not hear the sounds of the giggling.

But the Warren Tech guard's smile lasted only a moment. So, too, did the laughter from the fans wearing green.

Roy, chasing the guard, swerved and came up behind him at an angle. With a perfectly timed reach, he lifted the ball away in mid-dribble. The guard, his smile vanishing, stared at his empty hands. It was his turn to be confused and embarrassed. The crowd went silent, as if someone had thrown a switch.

Holding the ball in both hands, Roy looked around. He wore no smile of triumph, but he no longer wore the flush of embarrassment either. The usual blank expression was back in place. His teammates, shifting gears with the sudden change of events, broke into a dead run for the other end of the court. Roy looped a pass to Eddie, now at midcourt. Eddie took in the ball, dribbled once, and fired a two-handed pass toward the empty space under the basket. Jimmy, racing toward the corner, saw the ball in the air and cut sharply to his left. He caught the ball, dribbled once, and all alone under the basket, laid in the ball for a field goal.

Floyd was on his feet. He did not remember getting up, but he was standing, shooting a fist in the air, shouting when the ball dropped through the net.

Around him, the crowd was silent, stunned by the sudden development and the speed with which the Falcons had gotten a player and the ball down the court to cash in on the turnover. Then a giant roar from all around the arena rolled down onto the court. The people in green weren't cheering—but everyone else was.

Floyd caught Roy's eye in the moment before the Trojans brought the ball back into play. Gene was clapping him on the back. Floyd, smiling, clapped his hands together in Roy's direction. The boy clapped his hands together in return and ran over to take up his defensive position.

Floyd backed up and sat down on the bench again. He glanced at one of the huge scoreboards: Falcons 2, Trojans 0. And alongside Jimmy's name, he saw a 1 in the field-goal column and a 2 in the total-points column. The clock showed eleven seconds gone in the game. A long way yet to go.

Well, Floyd thought, they'll never be able to say that we trailed all the way.

From there to the end of the first quarter, the two teams swapped field goals and the lead. The Warren Tech guard with the reddish hair was neither so confidently fancy nor so arrogantly careless as he had been. The Trojans were giving nothing more away. They were a polished, disciplined, skilled basketball team. Their big center was every bit as good as he had been billed. Strong and quick, a good jumper, sure-handed with his tip-ins, he was giving Eddie the toughest game of his life. The forwards were a couple of sure-shot artists, and the two guards were, indeed, magicians when it came to ball handling.

But the Falcons were giving nothing away, either. Eddie battled the big center every step of the way. The twins were playing their best defense of the season. It was as if Roy's triumph was all the greater for coming in the wake of humiliation, and it had lifted both the twins to the heights. Their skittering feet and flickering hands repeatedly threw the Trojans off their stride. Jimmy, following his lay-up shot in the opening seconds, pumped in two shots from the corner. Gene Montgomery, although scoreless, was a bastion on defense, helping Eddie under the boards, and a steadying hand in the Falcons' attack.

The first ten minutes of the game clearly showed that the Trojans had the advantage—in height, strength, maybe even individual skill. But, equally clearly, the Falcons had an advantage of their own: With the exception of Jimmy, they all had played basketball with each other all of their lives, and they moved and thought as one on the basketball court.

At the buzzer ending the first quarter, the Trojans' advantages added up to a one-point lead, 10–9, over the Falcons.

As his players approached, Floyd slid a duffel bag out from beneath the bench and began extracting towels and passing them around.

From somewhere in the crowd across the court a voice rang out, "Go, Falcons!" Floyd, startled, looked in the direction of the shout, but he saw no one he recognized in the wall of faces.

He glanced down the sideline, and for a brief moment his eyes met those of the white-haired Warren Tech coach. "He knows that I know," Floyd said to himself, "that we can beat his team."

Floyd's hands had stopped shaking with the game's first field goal, Jimmy's lay-up following Roy's steal. His heartbeat had returned to normal. And now, passing out the towels, he felt a sense of confidence, almost calmness. The first quarter had proven that the Falcons were not doomed to take a thrashing. To the contrary, they were playing like winners.

Floyd looked around at his perspiring players.

Eddie, mopping his face with a towel, muttered, "That guy's tough."

"Move out on him," Floyd said. "Try to pull him out from under the boards. If he follows you out, then Jimmy"—he glanced at Jimmy, making sure the words were getting through—"can go under for lay-ups. If he doesn't follow you out, start shooting like you were a forward."

Eddie nodded.

"Defense is going to win this game," Floyd said. "If you get tired and have to rest out there, do your resting on offense, not defense. One lapse is two points for them. Their whole system is based on working the ball in slowly, waiting for you to make a mistake that enables them to score."

He turned to the twins. "You're doing great," he

said. "Keep it up." They nodded without speaking.

Floyd turned back to Eddie. "As for the big center, he plays rough, and he's going to be in foul trouble before the game is over," he said. He paused and half-grinned at his younger brother. "Make sure of it, will you?"

Eddie nodded, then repeated, "He's tough."

Floyd glanced down the sideline at the Trojans gathered in a circle around their coach. None of them was moving. They stood like statues, their eyes fixed on the figure in the center. He was jerking his head from side to side as he spoke, occasionally jabbing the air with a forefinger.

Floyd wondered what the Warren Tech coach was telling his players. There were bound to be adjustments. The Warren Tech Trojans, defending state champions, had not come to the tournament to have themselves scared silly, perhaps even defeated, by a team from Cedar—what?—Grove. The veteran coach with his two assistants would know what to do. They would know the moves, the changes, the tactics necessary to put the ragtag upstarts back in their place and send them packing for home. The time had come to score those precious points that come as a result of superior coaching. Floyd had seen it happen. He had seen veteran coaches, with the right change at the right time, turn a game around, and was now wondering what ingenious stroke was being developed on the other side of the scorer's table.

The buzzer signaling the start of the second quarter

interrupted his thoughts. Floyd and the players clasped hands in the center of the circle and pumped three times. "Get 'em," he said.

The Warren Tech coach's strategy became obvious immediately: slow down. The methodical Trojans became even more methodical. The deliberate style of attack became even more deliberate, the slow break slower than ever. Bernie Dodge had figured out, and rightly so, that his Trojans could not win trying to outrun the Falcons. The boys from Cedar Grove were too quick, and they had played together long enough to make the wild running and passing work. The way to win was to keep the ball out of the Falcons' hands, and to make sure that every possession netted a score. So the Trojans passed and passed and passed, and they dribbled and dribbled and dribbled, working for and waiting for the sure shot at the basket.

It was sound strategy. For the Falcons, the slow-down spelled trouble. A missed shot, if they failed to get the rebound against the big center, meant the loss of the ball for many precious seconds, perhaps even minutes. The Falcons' fast-break style of attack relied for success on taking a lot of shots. But they could not take shots if they did not have the ball. The slowdown also increased the chances of one or more of the Falcons getting into foul trouble trying to steal the ball.

Eddie's efforts to lure the big center out from under the boards worked. With the center a couple of steps out, Jimmy sailed through for a lay-up. Later, with the center hanging back, guarding the corridor under the boards, Eddie pumped in a shot from just inside the free-throw line. But the tactic, while it produced the Falcons' only two field goals of the second quarter, was not successful for long. The Trojans' forwards, each standing six feet four inches, moved in to fill the void under the boards when the center stepped out.

By halftime, the Trojans had widened the lead over the Falcons to 19–14.

"There's only one way, really, to stop a slowdown," Floyd said, "and that's to take the lead."

Floyd was standing in the middle of the dressing room. He nervously ran a hand through his hair. His other hand was stuffed in the hip pocket of his slacks.

Around him, the players were draped on the benches. Eddie was slumped forward, a towel around his shoulders. Jimmy was sprawled on his back, covering half the length of a bench, one knee raised, his right forearm over his eyes. Gene, leaning forward, stared at Floyd; there was no smile on his face this time. The twins both leaned back against a locker, breathing heavily.

Floyd searched the walls and the ceiling of the dressing room for the wisdom he needed. He kept talking, almost as if to himself. "If the Trojans were behind, it no longer would be to their advantage to let the seconds tick off the clock. They would need to score. The clock would be on our side, not theirs. They'd have to take their shots and their chances. We can beat 'em at that game. We need the lead—just once—and we can win."

31

"It's that big center," Eddie said softly, speaking more to himself than the others. "If we could just get him out of there—just for a few minutes . . ."

Floyd glanced at his brother. Eddie was right. The big center's strength under the boards, coupled with his sure-handed rebounding, was turning too many of the Falcons' offensive efforts into one-shot attempts. The Trojans were a good team—good at every position—but it was the center who provided the difference for them. Eddie was playing well, but he could not whip the big center consistently. The Falcons had to find a way to beat him, or pull him out of position, or get around him—or something. Success against the big center, even if only temporary, offered the only hope of taking the lead and breaking the Trojans' stifling slowdown.

"He's got three fouls," Gene said. "One more, the fourth, and he'll get cautious, and then . . ."

"Eddie's got three fouls, too," Floyd said. "One more and Eddie will get cautious."

The dressing room was silent. The walls offered Floyd no advice. Neither did the ceiling.

Then William Logan, sitting on the training table, said, "I don't have any fouls."

Again silence.

"Yeah," Floyd said slowly. He was smiling. "Yeah, I think that's it."

Four

The start of the second half was only moments away. Floyd, his team around him at the bench, leaned into the circle. He extended his hands. The players clasped their hands on his. They pumped three times and released. Nobody said anything.

The noise of the crowd, rolling down on the Falcons from all sides, was deafening.

The referee, ball in hand, walked toward the center of the court. The Falcons' second-half starters walked onto the court: William, Jimmy, Eddie, Gene, Ray.

Floyd backed up and sat down on the bench. Roy sat next to him. John Hartley and Bobby Watson were on the other side of Roy.

Floyd glanced across the scorer's table at the Trojans' bench. There were no signs that the Trojans' coaches had noticed the new player on the court for the Falcons. Or, if they had, they failed to recognize the significance of the change. Everything seemed like business as usual at the Warren Tech bench as the players took up their positions on the court. Eddie would make the center jump with William standing in at guard for Roy. Then the players would switch—William to center, Eddie to forward, Gene to guard with Ray—with Jimmy remaining in his forward slot. The changes were sure to come as a surprise to the Trojans.

Floyd reflected with a small smile that the changes had come as a surprise even to him. He recalled his earlier conclusion that the starters—unable to count on help from the bench—were going to have to carry the load all the way themselves. They offered the Falcons' only hope of victory. The Falcons' thin line of substitutes did not come close to matching the Trojans' bench strength. And yet, here was William Logan coming off the bench to take the court in the lead role of a major tactical move. If Floyd was surprised by the change, the Trojans were sure to be surprised, too.

Surely the element of surprise was worth a couple of points. Floyd hoped so. Trailing five points, the Falcons needed to score. But just as important, his players needed tangible proof their strategy was working.

Eddie and the big center stepped into the circle for the tip-off. Off to the side, a Warren Tech forward noticed the new player near him. He took William's measure, then turned his attention back to the two players flanking the referee in the circle.

Surely by now the Warren Tech coaches had noticed a new face in the Cedar Grove lineup. But they had no way of knowing the full impact of the change until the action got hot and heavy, too late for the luxury of a moment's thought about the necessary adjustments or for helpful words of advice.

The big center outjumped Eddie again. He flicked the ball back to the little guard with the reddish hair and raced toward his position under the basket. William picked him up along the way while Eddie backed off into a forward position and Gene slipped into the vacant guard spot.

Unlike Eddie, William, at six feet four inches, could not match the Warren Tech center's height. Neither was William as strong as Eddie. For sure, the strategy was a gamble. The Falcons were betting there was more to be gained than lost by weakening themselves at center. With no fouls, William was ready to play recklessly, tempting the center to respond with a recklessness of his own. Floyd watched the shorter, thinner William move up against the big center, and he felt a pang of doubt. The other player seemed to tower over William, making him look thinner than ever.

The big center blinked in surprise at William. He looked around for Eddie and found him moving out to meet a Trojan dribbler. Something was different, but why? The big player was frowning in puzzlement as William moved in close.

Floyd turned for a quick glance down the sideline at the Warren Tech bench. What he saw eliminated his brief flurry of doubt. The picture on the court was now clear for all to see, and Bernie Dodge was reading the implications of the change. He was getting to his feet, staring at the scene on the court. An assistant coach was rising beside him, saying something. Bernie Dodge was nodding. Floyd felt a sense of satisfaction, for the signs of concern on the Warren Tech bench served as an endorsement of his strategy. Floyd Bentley, the first-year coach fresh out of college, was worrying the veteran Bernie Dodge, who had been winning championships when Floyd was in grade school. Then Floyd felt a tinge of embarrassment. Why shouldn't he outsmart Bernie Dodge? He and his Falcons came here to win, didn't they? He thought of John Raymond and quickly turned his attention back to the action on the court.

The Trojans were backing off the assault and slowing their attack. They were sticking with the strategy of passing and passing and passing, dribbling and dribbling and dribbling, searching for the surefire opening for a field goal. And that opening quickly became obvious—a new Falcon center, two inches shorter and clearly not as strong as Eddie, was guarding their center under the basket.

The Trojan with the ball dribbled in place a moment, then sent a high pass toward the basket.

The big center went up. William went with him. He had William whipped. But the high pass skittered off the center's fingertips, bounced off the rim, and fell into the hands of Eddie, coming up to help with the rebound.

By the time Eddie planted his feet, with the ball held firmly in both hands, Gene was beside him.

Jimmy and William were racing full tilt for the other end of the court. Eddie handed the ball to Gene and followed Jimmy and William downcourt. Gene fired a long pass to Jimmy, and he took it on the run. He dribbled once and bounced a pass into empty space in front of Eddie, who was coming up from behind. William, running with Jimmy, swerved and screened out a Trojan defender heading for Eddie. Eddie grabbed the ball, went up, and laid the ball on the rim. It rolled lazily around the rim for six inches. Then it fell through.

The scoreboards at either end of the arena flickered the score change in lights: Falcons 16, Trojans 19.

Floyd was on his feet, his fist raised above his head, a wide smile on his face. The strategy of placing William Logan at the center position had in a way produced the field goal. The sight of the smaller, less powerful William at the center position had enticed the Trojans to try a high pass to their center, a chancier play than they usually liked. The weakening at center had paid off, and in a way that Floyd had never imagined. The field goal was a bonus. And now the Falcons trailed the Trojans by only three points.

The island of green in the bleachers across the court remained seated and mute. But around the rest of the arena, the fans were on their feet cheering. The roar of the crowd, punctuated by shouts of *"Falcons!"* startled Floyd for a moment. It was the roar of fans cheering their own team—his own team—on to victory. They had decided they wanted the Falcons in their faded pink shirts and faded gray trunks to beat the cocky, flashy defending champions. The team from Cedar Grove was knocking the best team in the Class A ranks into a reel. And the fans were loving it.

At the sideline, Floyd was waggling his hands in a signal to Gene and trying to shout above the roar of the crowd. Gene somehow heard him. He turned and looked at Floyd, then nodded in acknowledgment of the signal. He ran over and relayed the signal to Ray, and the two of them moved into a full-court press.

Maybe, just maybe, Floyd thought, the off-balance Trojans will lose their cool—if only for a second— with the surprise of guards waggling hands in their faces deep in the backcourt.

A Trojan guard managed to get the ball inbounds past Ray's waving arms and into the hands of his partner with the reddish hair. The fancy-dribbling guard turned and went into his act. He had the quickness and skill to get the Trojans out of trouble, but he never got started. Gene slapped out a hand and knocked the ball away. Ray and the other Warren Tech guard dived for the loose ball. Ray won and came out of the melee dribbling. He headed straight for the basket. Gene moved over a step, forcing the red-headed guard to swerve in his pursuit of Ray. The other guard, off balance, was out of the play. Ray had the moment of freedom he needed. He laid the ball up for a field goal.

Falcons 18, Trojans 19.

The crowd was roaring, *"Fal-cons!"*

Floyd, still on his feet, waved both arms in a

sweeping motion pointing upcourt, telling Gene and Ray to abandon the full-court press and drop back into position.

Bernie Dodge was on his feet, too, his arms forming a huge T, signaling for a time-out. His Trojans needed a field goal badly. But even more they needed to collect themselves. They needed to put the brakes on the Falcons' newfound momentum. They needed to regain control of the action. A player's shout to the referee, followed by a buzzer, stopped the clock and sent the players walking toward their benches.

Floyd stepped toward his approaching players and touched hands with each of them as they walked past, headed for the towels piled on the bench.

Standing in the center of the group, Floyd gave them a moment to catch their breath and towel off the perspiration. Ray, in the wake of his sensational play, was as blank-faced as ever. He might have been standing in the lunch line at Cedar Grove High for all the excitement he revealed. Gene was different. He was smiling, his eyes electric. He was experiencing the thrill of things working and sensing victory. Jimmy was watching Floyd without expression. His pass to Eddie for the first field goal of the half had been a brilliant play. "Nice going," Floyd said when their eyes met. Jimmy nodded. William and Eddie were staring into space, their jaws clenched tightly. Floyd glanced at the scoreboard, at the crowd, and at the Warren Tech bench, where Bernie Dodge was working his mouth, bobbing his head, and stabbing the air with a forefinger.

Floyd said, "Alertness pays off, doesn't it?" He smiled at the players around him, making sure he had their attention. "The Warren Tech stall is being called off at this very moment down there at their bench. We're back into a basketball game. We're still one point behind, but we've gotten close enough to put an end to the stall. They'll still be deliberate, careful, patient—that's their style. Don't fall into the trap of trying to play their kind of game. We'll play our own kind of game. Okay? We'll run 'em crazy. Understand?"

A couple of the players nodded.

"William, start pressing and press hard against their center. He'll press back. He plays rough. He won't be able to help himself. He'll press back, and he'll foul you. We need to get him started worrying about having four fouls. Or better still, sitting on the bench. You can afford a couple of fouls if you have to take them. Don't worry about it. But he can't afford even one more without getting himself into serious trouble."

William nodded his head as Floyd spoke. He understood his assignment. After all, the scheme had been his idea.

The buzzer ended the time-out.

Floyd managed to keep his seat on the bench as the two Warren Tech guards brought the ball upcourt. He could not help admiring them. They were good. He marveled at the way Ray and Roy, and now Ray and Gene, had succeeded in containing them. Both of them were masterful dribblers, capable of weaving through an entire team and laying in a field goal. So far, though, they had not been able to do it against the Falcons.

Gene and Ray moved out to oppose them.

The fans, sensing an upset victory by the team from—where?—Cedar Grove, and loving every minute of it, shouted in unison, "Get that ball! Get that ball!" The rhythmic chant seemed to rock the arena.

Crossing the center stripe, the guard with the reddish hair passed down the sideline to a forward. The forward faked a jump short, taking Jimmy with him, and sent a low pass in to the center under the basket. The center took in the pass beyond William's outstretched hands. He bounced the ball once and began his turn, going up for a hook shot. William, behind him, stood his ground. The center, turning and rising, caught William on the forehead with a forearm. William, arms akimbo, sprawled backward and fell to the floor out of bounds. Floyd almost smiled at William's bit of overacting.

The center continued upward and hooked the ball into the basket. But before it hit the nets the shrill whistle of the referee cut through the crowd noise.

Floyd kept himself seated on the bench. For a moment that seemed like an hour, he waited for the signal from the referee. The foul was either on the big center for charging or on William for blocking, depending on which player the referee considered to have rightful possession of the space where the collision occurred.

The referee waggled his hands, palms down—no

goal—and the big center lifted his hand to signal he was the guilty party.

The center looked at the bench. With a fourth foul logged against him, he had to be wondering whether he was staying in the game, to play cautiously, or going to the bench.

Behind him, William was getting to his feet with a helping hand from Eddie.

Five

After a flurry of conversation among the three coaches at the Warren Tech bench, the center stayed in the game with four fouls against him.

The players moved to the other end of the court and William stepped to the free-throw line.

The huge scoreboards read: Falcons 18, Trojans 19, and the clock showed the third quarter halfway gone.

The roar of the crowd rolled down onto the court from all around the bowl of seats. The fans, along with the players on the court and the coaches on the benches, sensed a turning point in the making.

At the Cedar Grove bench Floyd draped an arm around Roy's shoulder and leaned his head in close to the guard's ear. "You go back in for William now, right after the free throw," he said. The William Logan ploy had worked. Its purpose had been accomplished. William, unworried about getting himself into foul trouble, had succeeded in luring the Trojans' center into committing his fourth foul. Now he was sure to be overly cautious, timid, and tentative—duck soup for Eddie. This was going to be the payoff. It was time to collect the dividends. "We'll go back to our regular lineup now," Floyd said. Roy nodded and got to his feet, heading for the scorer's table to check in and be ready to take the court at the first break in the action after William's free throw.

William at the free-throw line bounced the ball twice. He eyed the basket. He took a deep breath. He pumped and fired. With the ball in the air, the arena was suddenly quiet. The shot had enough arch, and at the peak it looked good. But it was a fraction of an inch off to the right. The ball bounced off the rim. A loud moan—"*Ooooh*"—came from the fans who had taken the Falcons as their team in the battle against the defending champions.

Eddie leaped high and grabbed the ball. Falling away, he fired the ball back toward the basket. The shot missed. The Warren Tech center, coming up over William, got the rebound. But he turned quickly and his fingertips lost their hold. The ball slipped away and bounced out of bounds.

A buzzer sounded, and Roy trotted onto the court. William returned to the bench. Floyd got to his feet and stepped forward to greet him. They touched hands, nodding slightly to each other, and both sat down on the bench.

On the court the Falcons realigned themselves in their original positions—Eddie at center, Ray and Roy at guard, Gene with Jimmy at forward—and Roy

44

stood out of bounds under the Warren Tech basket with the ball, ready to resume play.

He zipped a pass inbounds to Jimmy at the side of the keyhole.

Floyd, seated on the bench and leaning forward, elbows on his knees, caught himself frowning. "This game isn't over yet," he told himself.

Jimmy took Roy's pass, jumped, fired, and— *swish!*—scored from fifteen feet out. The scoreboard blinked the change: Falcons 20, Trojans 19. The Falcons had caught the Trojans and passed them. They were in the lead for the first time since the opening minute of the game. The Trojans no longer could stall. They had to score. And to score, they had to shoot. The Falcons were back on track with their own style of play.

Seconds later, Ray lunged toward a Trojan pass, arm outstretched, and caught a piece of the ball, deflecting it toward Gene. Gene grabbed the loose ball. Jimmy, on his way downcourt at the moment of the deflection, raced along the sideline. Gene fired a pass half the length of the court, aiming at a spot under the basket. Jimmy veered from the sideline and took it in. He dribbled once and twirled the ball upward toward the basket. The ball dropped through without touching the rim.

Falcons 22, Trojans 19.

Then, with Eddie taking control of the boards against the Trojan center, now heavy-footed and tentative in his caution, the Falcons poured in two more field goals while yielding one to extend their lead to five points, 26–21.

The Warren Tech coach called another time-out.

Floyd, meeting his players at the bench, told them what he had been telling himself. "This game isn't over yet." But the players no more believed the words of caution than Floyd believed them himself. The Falcons had caught the Trojans when they had to do it. They were playing their own game, and it was working. The Trojans were in disarray, on the brink of desperation. The look of victory was in the eyes of every player standing around Floyd at the bench. Even the blasé Jimmy Gunn, breathing hard and toweling off perspiration, had a smile on his face, and he kept nodding his head as if someone were telling him that everything was going right. Even the dead-pan twins each wore a trace of a grin. The Falcons were winning, and they knew it.

When play resumed, Warren Tech's big center was gone from the court. His warm-up jacket draped over his shoulders, his head bowed low, he sat on the bench, staring at the floor. In his place on the court was a player not quite so tall, not quite so strong, and surely not quite so skilled. Floyd watched Eddie sizing up the newcomer.

"You outlasted the big gun, li'l brother," he mumbled to himself. "You whipped him."

From the first moment of play Eddie dominated the substitute center. Eddie had a reach advantage—an inch or more—and he made it pay off. He was the stronger of the two; and when they bumped, the Warren Tech substitute came off the worse for the experience. Eddie had him whipped in skill, too, leaving him behind with a masterful fake in their first encounter. With barely a minute gone, the signs of intimidation were clear. He started trying too hard to offset Eddie's reach advantage, losing his balance and almost fouling Eddie. He backed off from bruising physical contact, leaving Eddie free to move. And, hoping to avoid being faked out of position, he slowed his reactions to Eddie's movements. The substitute was not a poor player, but he was no match for Eddie, and Eddie powered his way over, around, and through him. The backboards belonged to the Falcons.

At the same time, the Falcons began to collect the dividends on a lifetime of playing together. The impossible passes were completed because both passer and receiver knew each other's abilities, limits, and inclinations. The instinctive knowledge of what a teammate was going to do next provided screens for shooters, lanes for dribblers. Jimmy, having played with his teammates only the one season, was outside the mystical connection that was producing miracles. But his jump shots and ball handling were every bit a part of the unstoppable force of the Falcons sailing through the fourth quarter.

Frustrated, the Trojans began to come apart at the seams. On defense, they flailed wildly and ineffectively. On offense, they took chances that no Warren

Tech team ever dreamed of taking. The coach with the silver hair was spending a lot of time standing at the sideline shouting directions at his players. In their desperation, the Trojans committed errors that no Warren Tech team, carefully coached in the art of errorless basketball, had ever committed in the past. And the Falcons grabbed every opportunity the Trojans handed them.

By the time the clock ticked into the final minute of play, the Falcons stood out front with an eleven-point lead, 44–33.

As the last minute ticked away, Floyd stood at the sideline. William Logan, John Hartley, and Bobby Watson stood with him.

The roar of the crowd swept down over them like an ocean wave, *"Fal-cons! Fal-cons!"*

Floyd squinted up at the clock on the scoreboard. Forty-one seconds to go.

On the court, the arc lights seemed to Floyd to be brighter, more brilliant than before. The whole scene was a mirror, almost blinding. The arena was uncomfortably warm. Floyd was perspiring. He wiped his forehead. His hands were shaking again. He thrust them in his hip pockets and stared at the action in front of him.

Thirty seconds remaining.

Roy passed the ball to Gene. Gene dribbled in place, near the sideline. He passed the ball back out to Roy. Roy dribbled and stared impassively at the Warren Tech defender in front of him.

Fifteen seconds.

Roy passed across the court to Ray. Ray passed downcourt to Jimmy.

Ten seconds.

Jimmy stood in place, dribbling slowly, eying his guard.

The crowd picked up the count on the clock with a roar. *Nine, eight, seven, six, five, four.*

Jimmy leaped and fired the ball toward the basket. *Two . . . one.*

The ball bounced off the rim, a miss. It didn't matter. The buzzer sounded. The game was over.

Floyd let out a whoop and threw both hands in the air. Needing one more bit of confirmation, he glanced at one of the scoreboards and saw *Falcons* flashing off and on in the computerized scoreboard's signal that the game had a winner: the Cedar Grove Falcons.

The court suddenly was swarming with fans. Floyd ran into the crowd, looking for his players. The crowd had swallowed them up. He could not see a single red shirt with black trim. Milling and shoving his way through the people, with strangers slapping him on the back and reaching out to shake his hand, Floyd found himself suddenly facing the Warren Tech coach. The man's white hair was a little mussed. His face was a little redder. With obvious effort, he was managing a smile.

"Great game, Coach Bentley," Bernie Dodge said, extending his right hand. "You've got a great bunch of kids."

Floyd wiped a sweaty palm on his trousers, took the extended hand, and pumped. "Thanks," he said.

"You've got a great team. We were lucky to win."

"Luck had nothing to do with it," the Warren Tech coach said. And then he was gone.

Floyd spotted Eddie towering above the crowd, and Eddie saw him. The brothers ran toward each other and embraced. Eddie had fought a hard battle against a stronger and more skillful player, and in the end he had won.

Gene, his red hair plastered to his forehead with perspiration, was laughing and shouting something while his beaming parents stood by. Gene's father extended a hand and said, "Congratulations, Floyd." Floyd shook his hand, and then shook Gene's hand. "We beat the city slickers," he told Gene. Gene laughed.

Floyd saw Jimmy in the crowd. He was grinning broadly while taking a handshake from one of the Warren Tech players, the fancy-dribbling guard with the reddish hair. The two boys had the same haircut. Jimmy's faded shirt looked flat alongside the bright green one. Floyd watched them and wondered what Jimmy thought of farmer clothes now.

The twins, standing together as always, appeared more exhausted and perhaps relieved than jubilant. Grinning slightly, they were still breathing heavily. They seemed uable to believe the game had ended. For them, it had been an unending series of the start-stop-start-stop maneuvers of guards trying to bottle up a pair of expert ball handlers. They had done the job.

The swirling crowd on the court was beginning to thin out, and Floyd began rounding up his players to head for the dressing room.

As they walked off the court toward the ramp leading to the dressing room, two other teams were moving toward the court to begin their warm-up time before the second game. One of them would become the Falcons' opponent the next night.

Uniformed ushers moved onto the court to steer the remaining fans back to their seats while the two teams waited at the sideline.

Floyd, stepping into the ramp behind his players, turned and glanced up at the scoreboard one more time: 44–33.

Floyd had only a moment alone with his players in the dressing room, the door locked against the mob of people in the corridor.

"You're going to have letter jackets," he told the players, "if I have to sell my van to pay for them."

The players at Cedar Grove High never got letter jackets. The school did not provide them. Some parents were able to afford an unnecessary garment for their sons, and some were not. Down through the years, an unspoken custom developed—if everyone could not have a letter jacket in red and black, then no one was going to have one. Mothers stitched the CG emblem on a jacket at hand. Floyd's own letters were on mackinaw jackets, none of which he had worn since graduation.

Somebody said, "Okay!"

Floyd caught the sharp look of surprise on Jimmy's face. Yes, the boy from the big school outside Houston probably figured a letter jacket was an automatic reward at the end of the season. Didn't lettermen always get jackets? They did where he came from. Floyd returned Jimmy's stare. The boy from the big city still had some things to learn about Cedar Grove High.

"Hey, Floyd," Gene piped up. "Are you sure your old van is worth enough to buy jackets for all of us?"

Floyd smiled and without answering walked to the door and opened it to the crowd in the corridor.

The dressing room was emptying now, becoming quiet. The last shouted cheer, led by Gene, died out. The last parents left.

Gene's father, shaking Floyd's hand again, grinned and said, "I can't wait to get to the window table at Big John's with all those coffee drinkers in the morning."

Floyd returned the smile. "Tell 'em we don't feel embarrassed at all."

The last of the strangers were pumping Floyd's hand and edging toward the door. A couple of them, he was sure, were college coaches. In the milling and shouting and confusion inside the crowded dressing room, he hadn't caught their names. It didn't matter.

The television crew, with a camera riding on a shoulder, backed out of the room. The last reporter asked, "When did you start thinking you could beat Warren Tech?" Floyd replied for the last time, "When the final buzzer sounded."

Finally, only one outsider remained, Don Benson, the executive secretary of the Arkansas Athletic Association and the guiding hand of the tournament. He was beaming his congratulations to the dressing room as a whole.

"The college coaches were enormously impressed by Eddie's play," he said, talking to Floyd. But as he spoke, he turned to Eddie and gave an enthusiastic nod of approval.

It seemed to Floyd that the room grew quiet. Everyone was listening. "The place is swarming with college coaches out doing their talent scouting," Benson went on. "It's the same every year. You can imagine."

"I guess so," Floyd said.

"Really enormously impressed by Eddie's play," he repeated. "The way he handled that big Warren Tech center—really something." He paused, then added almost as an afterthought, "Impressed by you, too, Coach Bentley, the way you handled your team."

Floyd felt the eyes of his players on him and almost flinched. The past week's chatter around Cedar Grove came back to him like a rebroadcast.

"Well," Floyd said finally with a shrug, "I hope we can impress all of them again tomorrow night."

Benson nodded, still smiling. "Where are you and your boys staying tonight?"

"Staying?" Floyd repeated. He felt a sudden emptiness in his stomach.

"Yes. You have reservations someplace, haven't you?"

Floyd's face went blank. The dressing room suddenly seemed very, very quiet.

Six

"I've got to find us a place," Floyd said.

Don Benson blinked at him. "You don't have reservations?" he asked. His voice carried a tone of disbelief.

Floyd remembered the telephone call from Benson after the Falcons won the district tournament and a berth in the state finals. Benson had blocked out motel rooms for each of the eight teams in the final round. He had wanted to assign the Falcons to a motel and confirm the number of rooms needed. But Floyd planned to drive them home to Cedar Grove if they lost. And, having just learned that the Falcons' first-game opponent was last year's defending champion, Warren Tech, losing seemed to be a very real possibility. The murmurings of the townspeople, and some of the players, too, that the Falcons were foolhardy victims being led to the slaughter by an ambitious inexperienced coach did not help bolster his optimism. No, Floyd figured, there was no sense in spending the school's money needlessly. And, he could not help telling himself, there was no point in giving Big John Raymond one more argument. If the Falcons lost, they would ride home in Floyd's van after the game. If they won, well, there would be time then to find overnight accommodations. That was the way the teams in the Class B tournament did it. So what was so different? No problem.

But something in Don Benson's expression and in the tone of his voice alarmed Floyd.

Something in the silence of the unmoving players around him was bothersome, too.

"Is it a problem?" Floyd asked. He feared he already knew the answer.

Benson frowned. "This is a good-sized university," he said, "but this is not a large town." He paused. "The whole area is booked solid for the tournament every year."

A couple of players moved, heading for the showers. One was Jimmy Gunn. Floyd wished it had been any other player. Jimmy, and Gene with him, walked past Floyd and Don Benson into the shower room. The others followed, nobody speaking.

"It's a three-hour drive back to Cedar Grove," Floyd said slowly, thinking out loud. He looked at his watch—almost nine-thirty—and calculated the early-morning hour he would be delivering his players to their homes. "And three hours back here for tomorrow night's game."

"You don't want to do that," Benson said.

"I don't know what else to do."

"I don't know, either, to tell you the truth," Benson said. "But let me do some checking."

Floyd nodded absently.

"Wait here until you hear from me," Benson said. "I'll see what I can do, if anything."

"Okay. And thanks."

Benson left.

Floyd sat down on the training table. He heard the showers in the next room and occasionally a voice saying something he could not understand. A deep frown creased his forehead. The excitement of entering the Class A tournament and playing against the best had started turning sour before the Falcons even arrived. Now the electricity of defeating the Warren Tech Trojans was gone. The sourness was back, heavier than ever. He felt a tinge of embarrassment—he was a small-town coach who did not know how to act at the big-city tournament. He felt embarrassed for his players. And he wondered what Big John Raymond would say now. Big John had predicted embarrassment. Floyd dreaded the stares of his players and, from Jimmy Gunn, maybe remarks.

The players were coming out of the showers, dripping, and picking up towels from the training table and heading for their lockers.

"Don't we have anyplace to stay tonight?" one of the twins asked.

Floyd looked up. Of course, there had been chatter in the showers. All the players had heard the conversation between Floyd and Don Benson and knew the problem. Now they all were wondering what was going to happen.

Eddie was behind the twin. "Are we going to have to drive back to Cedar Grove tonight, and then drive back up here tomorrow?"

Floyd shrugged. "I don't know," he said. "We'll see. They're trying to find us something. We ought to know in a little while." After a pause, he added, "They'll come up with something."

Jimmy walked by without speaking, knotting a towel around his waist. Floyd watched him. He could imagine him contrasting last year and this year in his mind. Jimmy had remarked on the contrast enough times during the season. Now Floyd's imagination had no trouble carrying the contrast to absurdity. A year ago, Jimmy Gunn's team probably flew by chartered jet to the Texas state high-school tournament, with each player having his own corner suite in some elegant hotel, and steak for breakfast delivered by room service. And don't forget the fancy game uniforms, complete with glittering warm-up suits. Floyd bit his lip and looked away from Jimmy.

The last of the players, Gene and the other twin, came out of the showers. Their expressions asked the same question, but they said nothing.

From above the dressing room, the roar of the crowd announced the start of the second game, the two teams vying for a place in the semifinals against the Falcons. Floyd wanted to watch the game. He needed to see the Falcons' next opponent in action.

Maybe Don Benson would return quickly with good news. Then Floyd could deposit the team at a motel and return for at least part of the game. He did not want them to see it. Only two things could come out of the players watching tomorrow night's opponent, and both were bad: a case of the nerves about the talent coming up against them, or overconfidence in their ability to handle the team they were watching. Maybe he could leave them in the dressing room and step to the end of the ramp and watch the game. No, that did not sound like a good idea.

Gene's voice broke the long silence in the dressing room. "Did you think we were going to lose?" he asked. He spoke the words softly, his face serious.

Floyd glanced at Gene. Then he looked at the other players. Clearly, Gene's question was in the mind of every one of them—Jimmy, the twins, even Eddie.

Floyd knew the answer his players believed, that deep down, subconsciously, he must have thought the Falcons were going to lose. How could they defeat the mighty Warren Tech Trojans, defending Class A champions and only twice-beaten in the regular season? If Floyd did not believe the Falcons were going to lose, why had he allowed himself to drift into the single plan of driving home after the game?

Floyd frowned. He had never consciously admitted the possibility of losing, even to himself, but maybe the players were right. The thought worried him.

He took a deep breath, watching the waiting play-

59

ers. "Look," he said finally, "I've never gone into a game—as player or as coach—believing my team would lose. Anybody can beat anybody. We all know that." He paused and nobody said anything. "I didn't make reservations because I figured we could drive back home if we lost or find rooms if we won." He saw the frowns forming around him. "That's not saying that we were going to lose. In my senior year at Cedar Grove High, we went to the state Class B tournament, and this is the way we did it. No trouble. Nobody assumed we were going to lose just because we planned to drive home if we lost. So I figured we'd do the same thing here." He sighed. "Only thing, the whole area is booked."

Floyd was met by silence. The players resumed dressing.

"Dumb," he said finally, "but that's where we are."

There was a knock at the dressing-room door, and then it opened and Don Benson stepped inside, closing it behind him. He glanced at the questioning faces around him and walked across the room to Floyd.

"It looks like there isn't a single vacant room within fifty miles of town," he said. "And you can't just start driving around in the middle of the night looking for a place to stay."

Floyd nodded slowly. The players were edging in around the two of them, listening. Floyd avoided their eyes.

"But I've made an arrangement for you," Benson continued. "It's a bit unorthodox, but it's better than driving home to Cedar Grove tonight and back here tomorrow." He paused. "You can sleep here. The university's athletic department is agreeable."

"Here?" Floyd was not sure he understood. Surely not in the dressing room. Then where? Perhaps Benson had located dormitory space on the campus. Maybe some of the students were going to double up to make room. "You mean, on the campus?" he asked.

Don Benson seemed to correctly read Floyd's first interpretation of "here." "No, no, not here in the dressing room," he said quickly. Then he added, "And not exactly what you would call on the campus. It's simply too late in the evening to make those kinds of arrangements—crowding into a dormitory or a fraternity house."

"Well . . . ?"

"You can sleep here in the field house. The athletic department has tumbling mats. They'll do for beds, reasonably comfortable ones, I think. And you can use blankets from the football team. You'll be warm and . . . well, as I said, reasonably comfortable, I think. Maybe the basketball court itself would be the best place." He paused and smiled again. "What do you think? Beats making the trip to Cedar Grove and back again, doesn't it?"

Floyd was silent a moment. He thought of the three-hour drive to Cedar Grove, delivering his players to their homes in the wee hours after midnight. And then the three-hour drive back to Talbott State. Yes, the idea sounded better than a round trip.

"I'm afraid that's the best I can offer at this late hour," Benson said.

Floyd looked around at the players. "What do you think?"

Eddie shrugged and said, "Okay by me."

The twins shrugged and said nothing.

Gene, with a slight grin, piped up with, "I get dibs on the free-throw line."

Somebody else said, "Yeah, sure."

Jimmy Gunn said nothing.

Floyd turned to Benson. "Okay," he said, "we'll do it. And thanks. We sure appreciate all your help. We hate to be so much trouble."

"No trouble," Benson said with a nod. "That's what I'm here for. Just sorry I couldn't do better." He turned to the players. "You boys played a terrific game and beat a great team. You should be very proud. Good luck the rest of the way."

He shook hands with Floyd and turned toward the door, then turned back to face Floyd. "Oh, by the way . . ."

"Yes?"

"I'm sure I'll be able to nail down some rooms for you tomorrow night," he said. "Some people are going to be going home earlier than expected." He smiled. "The Warren Tech fans, for instance."

Floyd nodded. "Thanks," he said.

Benson left, closing the door; and Floyd turned back to the players. He opened his mouth to speak, but never got the words out.

"The floor!" Jimmy blurted. "You've got to be kidding! We don't even have rooms to sleep in! We've come to the state tournament and we're going to sleep on the basketball court!"

Stunned, Floyd stared at him.

"Good grief!" Jimmy muttered. The tone of disgust was unmistakable.

"Why don't you just shut up!" one of the twins said.

Floyd turned and stared at the boy who had spoken. Which one was he, Ray or Roy? Without their uniform numbers, Floyd could not tell them apart.

"Hang on, now!" Floyd barked. The dressing room fell silent. "You," he said, pointing a finger at the twin. "And you," he said, moving his finger to point at Jimmy. "And everyone else—"

"You always think you're so big and swell," the twin snapped, breaking off Floyd's words in midsentence.

"Quiet!" Floyd said. He was almost shouting.

But the twin didn't stop. Instead his voice rose to a shout. "We beat the big swells out there tonight but good. We beat *your* kind of team. You should have been on *their* team with your fancy haircut and your fancy clothes and then we'd have beaten you. What do you think of that?"

Short of trying to clap a hand over the twin's mouth, Floyd had been unable to think of a way of stopping the attack.

The twin, appearing on the brink of tears, was breathing heavily.

"Okay, now," Floyd said, almost gently, trying to calm everyone.

Jimmy's mouth was open. No sound came out. He gaped at the twin speechlessly.

Throughout the season, Jimmy's barbed remarks about the faded uniforms, the drafty dressing rooms, the cramped gymnasiums—all had gone unchallenged. True, his crack about John Hartley's farmer clothes had almost provoked a fight, but it had been a personal remark and John had taken it personally. The derogatory remarks about Cedar Grove High had always sent the players into a defensive shell of silence.

Until this night. Now the months of pent-up anger had boiled over. Now of all times, in the wake of probably the biggest victory in the basketball history of Cedar Grove High. Now on the eve of the second do-or-die game in the tournament.

"Look, I'm the dumb one," Floyd said finally, breaking the cold quiet of the dressing room. "It's my fault. Blame me."

He cast his eyes around the circle of players. "Okay?" he asked.

Nobody answered.

Floyd took a deep breath. "Let's go out and watch the game," he said. Mentally crossing his fingers, he added, "A little advance scouting never hurt anyone."

Eddie led the way, and the others followed.

Gene, walking through the door, rolled his eyes and said, "Yeah. After all, they're playing in our bedroom."

Nobody laughed.

Seven

Finally, the players were quiet, sleeping soundly.

Floyd raised himself to a sitting position on the tumbling mat and locked his hands around his knees. He stared through the gloom of the cavernous arena across the row of sleeping players. The only light shone from the exit ramps leading under the rows of seats.

In the silence, Floyd could hear the even breathing of his players. They were covered by the gray-and-green blankets of the Talbott State University football team. Their heads rested on seat cushions.

The time was a few minutes after midnight.

Floyd wanted to sleep. The day had been long. By now, the Cedar Grove High pep rally to give the team a send-off seemed light years away. Floyd could remember the cheers and the final wave as he and the team boarded his van for the drive to Talbott State. He could remember searching the faces in the crowd for John Raymond and not finding him. But all the rest was a blur, so far away. The three-hour drive from Cedar Grove through the murky, wintry weather had not only been wearying but worrisome. In the deathly quiet of the van, Floyd kept hearing John Raymond's warning: "You're going to take our boys up there and get them embarrassed in front of everybody." The silence of the players riding along in the van seemed ominous. Were they thinking the same thing? And then, after finally arriving at Talbott State, the game—the most tension-packed hour in Floyd Bentley's life. He was drained, exhausted, but wide awake.

There was another long, busy day ahead for him. Floyd needed to talk to coaches whose teams had played the Melville Heights Bulldogs. Floyd and his players had watched them win their way into the semifinals. The Bulldogs were impressive in thrashing the Williamstown Hornets. Floyd had learned a lot about the Falcons' next opponents by watching the game. But there was more to be known than was revealed in one game, especially when it was an easy runaway victory. There were tactics the Bulldogs liked to use but did not need tonight against the Williamstown Hornets. There were weaknesses to be exploited, but not by the helplessly outgunned Williamstown Hornets. Coaches of the teams who had played the Bulldogs knew these things, and Floyd needed to talk to them. There was a way—somehow—to beat them and he had to find it. He had a lot of telephone calls to make in the morning, a lot of work to do.

Floyd's mind went back to Cedar Grove, where by now everyone knew the final score: Falcons 44, Trojans 33.

The Falcons had not been humiliated. The boys in the faded uniforms, led by a young, inexperienced coach, had covered themselves with glory. They had knocked off mighty Warren Tech.

"John Raymond, you should have been here to see it," Floyd mumbled half aloud. But he knew what Big John and some of the others would be saying over their coffee tomorrow morning: "A fluke, that's all. Warren Tech had drawn a team that nobody ever heard of to play in the first round, and they were overconfident and not ready. The Falcons won't be so lucky next time. This Melville Heights outfit will be ready for them." A few of the coffee drinkers were bound to come to the defense of Floyd and the Falcons. Somebody was sure to say, "Aw, c'mon, beating Warren Tech anytime is a pretty big assignment, and the Falcons did it." And Big John was sure to reply, "Wait and see. Just wait and see." Big John Raymond did not easily change his mind. He had decreed humiliation for the Falcons and assigned the blame to Floyd. And what Big John decreed, Big John expected to see happen.

Floyd mulled over the words his imagination had put into Big John's mouth. They were true. Floyd had to admit it. Warren Tech, the powerful defending champion, had been cocky and confident taking the court against the little-known team from Cedar

Grove. The Falcons had surprised them, and in the end had beaten them. There would be no surprise in the next game. The Melville Heights Bulldogs would not be cocky and overconfident. They knew about the Cedar Grove Falcons.

Floyd glanced at the sleeping players and wondered what they had thought of the Melville Heights Bulldogs. They had seen the game. They had watched the Bulldogs race with wild abandon down the court, seemingly with no pattern, firing their shots on the run. They had seen how many of the crazy shots dropped—*swish!*—through the nets. They had watched the Bulldogs shift the action from the backcourt to the forecourt in the blink of an eye with a daring pass the length of the court. They had seen the accuracy of those passes, and the sure-handedness of the receivers, who pulled them in on fingertips, bringing the ball down to a dribble. They had seen tomorrow night's opponent, and now they had almost twenty-four hours to think about what they had seen.

Before going to sleep, the Falcons had been full of chatter about the Melville Heights Bulldogs.

"Man, they're the runningest team I ever saw," said Gene Montgomery, obviously impressed. "I thought we were a running team, but those guys are really wild."

Gene, for all his easygoing ways, was difficult to read. Floyd had always believed that inside there was a toughness to him, giving the lie to the laughter and the joking wisecracks he offered to the world. Gene had been impressed by the Bulldogs. He admitted as much. Was he frightened by them? Probably not, but Floyd could not tell for sure.

One of the twins said, "Well, they don't have anyone who can dribble like those Warren Tech guards."

The other twin agreed, "Uh-huh."

Because of their youth, Floyd figured that Roy and Ray were the most vulnerable of the Falcons to a case of nerves. But they had overcome the jitters caused by a giant arena filled with sixteen thousand thundering fans. They had recovered quickly from the jolt of the Warren Tech dribbler's first dazzling display of ball handling. Perhaps they could survive twenty-four hours of thinking about the Melville Heights Bulldogs.

"They know how to shoot," Eddie said. Then after a pause he added, "Lay-ups and outside stuff."

Eddie's words revealed that he, like Floyd, had spotted the weakness of the Melville Heights Bulldogs: the center position. Their center was gangly, unskilled, and at least three inches shorter than Eddie. Eddie was sure to win the battle of the boards.

"C'mon," Floyd had said finally. "Let's roll out the mats and get some sleep."

Earlier, as Floyd lay on the mat, and now as he sat staring into the shadows, he was not thinking about the Melville Heights Bulldogs, or John Raymond, or about the triumph over Warren Tech. Nor was he charting ways to cash in on Eddie's superiority tomorrow night. He was hearing again Jimmy Gunn's blurted exclamation—"The floor!"—and the angry snap of the twin's words, "You always think you're so big and swell!"

The exchange presented Floyd with a bigger challenge than the game plan for Melville Heights, and threatened more danger for the Falcons than the crazy shots of the Bulldogs. The words worried Floyd, and they would not leave his mind.

He glanced out over the row of sleeping boys and his eyes came to rest on the twins, side by side, both curled up under the blankets, identical even in sleeping posture. Unconsciously, he shifted his gaze to Jimmy Gunn, only the top of his head visible outside the gray-and-green blanket.

Floyd frowned. The conflict simmering beneath the surface for all these weeks had erupted into the open. Finally, a sneering remark by Jimmy had sparked a snarling retort from a teammate. Now with the season just two games—or maybe even one game—from ended, the resentment was no longer a dangerous undercurrent. The words had been spoken.

Through the season the victories had somehow patched over the differences. Winning had a way of smoothing out the frayed edges. The newcomer's sneering remarks were easier to take when he pumped in a dozen points and the Falcons were the winners. And Jimmy, too, was swept up in the excitement of victory, seeming at times not to notice the faded uniforms, the tiny gyms, the cramped dressing rooms. Occasionally, Floyd thought he saw signs that Jimmy was experiencing a change of heart. The twins' backcourt play, Eddie's strength under the basket, Gene's steady floor play—all these things drew cheers from Jimmy as well as from the others. But then another sneer, another remark, and the bubble burst, leaving Floyd to content himself with the fact that open warfare had not broken out.

Now, though, the words had been spoken.

This time victory, even over the vaunted Warren Tech Trojans, had not patched over the differences. No, the lid was off now.

The timing could not have been worse. Early in the season, or even midway through, there was time to repair a rift. Back then, a loss or two was affordable. But now, in the tournament, there was no time; no loss was affordable.

Floyd ran a hand through his hair. All through the season he had tried to handle the situation by attempting to keep the conflict beneath the surface. Maybe he should have brought it to a head early in the season. That might have settled matters and cleared the air. But, no, Floyd did not believe that. An explosion early in the season might have driven Jimmy off the team. That would have harmed Jimmy, and also would have harmed the players who drove him away. No, Floyd knew he had been right in trying to stave off an eruption. Yet the long-ticking bomb now had exploded at the most critical moment of the season. His own stupidity in mishandling the lodging arrangements had sparked the explosion. There was nothing to be done about that now, but was another bomb ticking?

The next flare-up was sure to be bad, perhaps in

the morning at breakfast, or during the campus tour the teams were taking in the afternoon, or in the dressing room before the game, or even on the court. There would be no Melville Heights–Williamstown game to capture the players' attention and take their minds off an angry exchange. No night of sleep to serve as a cooling-off period. No dream of playing in the championship game. There would be only the instant disintegration of the Cedar Grove Falcons basketball team.

Floyd stretched out on the tumbling mat again, pulled up the gray-and-green blanket, and closed his eyes.

Before dropping off to sleep, he decided that one of his calls tomorrow morning—the first call—would be to Saudi Arabia. A man he hardly knew, a man he had met only once, who was directing a construction project a half world away, seemed to hold the only possible hope of a solution. He was the man who had convinced Jimmy to give basketball a try at Cedar Grove High. He was the man who had fished with Jimmy and had camped with him. He was a man Jimmy Gunn listened to. Maybe Joe Gunn could make his son listen one more time.

Finally, Floyd slept.

Eight

Floyd awoke before dawn. The ramp lights cast their
yellowish beams faintly into the darkness on the basketball court. He raised himself to a sitting position.
Along the row of players, nobody stirred. They were
all sleeping soundly beneath the blankets. One of
them was snoring gently. Otherwise, all was silent.

Quietly, Floyd got to his feet. He locked his hands
behind his neck and stretched. He had not slept well.
Time and again through the night, he had half wak-
ened with terrible dreams unfolding in front of him.
In one, the Melville Heights Bulldogs were running
up and down the court at will, grabbing rebounds and
scoring field goals while the Falcons stumbled along
behind them, helpless. In another, four of the Falcons—Roy, Ray, Gene, and yes, Eddie, too—stopped
in midplay and pointed their fingers at Jimmy until
he ducked his head and walked off the court. Jimmy's
father was in one dream, seated at a desk, talking on a
telephone. Desert sands were visible behind him. He

was saying to Floyd, "If you were not so incompetent, you would be able to handle this problem with Jimmy without bothering me." Then there was one with a frowning Big John Raymond. He was sitting alone in the office where the school board had hired Floyd last summer. Big John did not speak. He just sat there, frowning.

After each terrible scene, Floyd drifted back into sleep.

Now he rubbed his eyes, and walking softly, headed for the ramp leading to the dressing room. He showered, shaved, and dressed quickly. He wanted to be back on the court when his players started waking up.

Walking out of the dressing room and turning toward the court, Floyd admitted to himself that he feared the day. Not the telephone scouting of the Melville Heights Bulldogs nor the preparation of the game plan. Certainly, not the game itself. Not even the telephone call to Saudi Arabia. But he feared the unavoidable periods during the day when the players would be left to themselves. He had important work to do, and he could not be with the players every minute of the day to stand guard, ready to quell a new outbreak of trouble. He dreaded the prospect of an explosion. Bad enough if he were on hand to intervene. But without him present, another eruption surely would wreck the Falcons. The team would fall apart, and there would be no time for regrouping. A team divided was no longer a team. It would be the end.

The lights in the ramps were turned off now and daylight, murky and dim, covered the court as Floyd walked out of the ramp and onto the court.

Gene was sitting up, rubbing his eyes. Jimmy was standing, stretching his arms above his head. The twins were moving under their blankets. One of them raised his head and looked around. Eddie was still sleeping.

Floyd forced a smile as he approached. "Well, how was it, spending the night in the Ritz?" he asked.

Gene said, "Swell. No problem."

Jimmy said, "Okay."

Floyd eyed Jimmy for a moment. Jimmy was looking out at nothing, staring into space as he stretched the kinks out. Then Floyd said, "Head on into the dressing room, everybody. The water's hot and feels great." He walked over to Eddie, bent down, and shook his shoulder gently. "C'mon, little brother. Time to rise and shine."

First Gene and Jimmy, and then the others, trailed off toward the dressing room, and Floyd followed them in. He sat on the training table while they showered and dressed.

From there, coats buttoned up around their necks, they walked out the front door of the field house and headed across the campus to the Student Union for breakfast. Special tables were being set up for the teams.

Floyd dropped back several paces. "Eddie," he said.

Eddie turned, and Floyd crooked his finger in a

gesture for Eddie to join him. Eddie dropped back and fell in step with his brother.

Floyd watched the other players, strung out along the sidewalk in front of them. Nobody was paying any attention. "You've got to make sure there's no more trouble today," he said.

"I'll try, but—"

"You're a senior, the only senior starter on the team, and they all look to you for leadership."

Eddie sighed. "I know."

"There's going to be a lot of time I'm not around. I've got work to do, phone calls about this Melville Heights outfit, a game plan to draw up."

"I said that I'd try."

Floyd glanced sharply at his younger brother. "You've got to do it."

"It's just that I can't guarantee what Jimmy's going to say next." Eddie paused. "You know, Floyd, I don't like his attitude any more than anyone else."

Ahead of them, the players were going up the steps and through the front door of the Student Union.

Floyd stopped. Eddie stopped with him.

"There's a lot riding on your success," Floyd said.

"I know. I'll try."

"Try to be upbeat with them. Try to keep anything from getting started. But if something does get started, move in and stop it right away."

"Okay," Eddie said. Then he added, "It'll be okay."

"Good."

Floyd and Eddie followed the players inside and

down the stairs to the basement cafeteria. After making sure they were in line at the hot table for their food and locating their seats, Floyd got himself a large Styrofoam cup of coffee and headed back to the field house. Breakfast, he figured, was probably the safest time to leave the players on their own. They were hungry, so were sure to be eating, not squabbling. And Floyd needed to get his hands on a telephone.

"Mrs. Gunn?"

Floyd was seated at a desk in a tiny office around the corner from the dressing room in the field house. The office was his for the day.

"Yes." The woman's voice came over the line from Cedar Grove.

"This is Floyd Bentley. I hope I didn't wake you."

"No." Then, after a pause, "Is something wrong, Coach Bentley?"

Floyd stared at the wall across from him. Of course something was wrong. Equally certain, Mrs. Gunn knew something was wrong. She knew of Jimmy's distress at moving from the huge Texas school to tiny Cedar Grove, and his opinion of the school, the coach, his teammates. She knew, too, of her husband's conversation with Floyd last October. So she had to know Floyd was not calling just to wish her a good morning.

Floyd chose his words carefully. "Nothing serious," he said, trying to sound like he meant it, "but I have

78

an idea that I think would be helpful for everyone, Jimmy and everyone else. And I . . ."

"Yes?"

"I'd like to give Mr. Gunn a call in Saudi Arabia and ask him to call Jimmy and, well, just wish him luck. It would be a great morale boost. Certainly for Jimmy. But for the rest of the players, too."

The line was silent for a moment. Floyd hoped she would not press him—"Is something wrong?"—for his reasons. He sensed that she knew she was not getting the whole story. Was she going to demand it? Floyd hoped not. He told himself that he had not really told a lie, since the problem, as he said, was not serious. Not yet, anyway. And he did want the telephone call from Saudi Arabia for morale purposes. That was the truth.

Finally, she said, "That sounds like a great idea."

Floyd sighed in relief.

Mrs. Gunn gave him the telephone number. "And," she added, "don't forget that they are eight hours ahead of us over there."

Floyd thanked her and hung up. He sat with his hand on the telephone for a moment and glanced at his watch. Seven-thirty. He calculated the time in Saudi Arabia. Three-thirty. He picked up the receiver and dialed the international operator.

The voice that answered the telephone in Saudi Arabia—obviously American with a touch of a southern accent—came through loud and clear, as if the person were speaking from the next room.

No, Joe Gunn was not available. He was at the construction site several miles away. There were no telephones there. Was it an extreme emergency? If so, a driver could be dispatched. Mr. Gunn would return quite late, if at all. He might spend the night at the construction-crew's quarters instead. He frequently stayed overnight at the site. Was there a message?

Floyd's heart sank. "No," he said, "no message." Then he quickly reversed himself. "Yes, there is a message." He gave his name and the number on the telephone in front of him. "And please tell Mr. Gunn"—he paused—"that while it is important that I speak with him as soon as possible, there is no cause for alarm."

Floyd replaced the receiver in its cradle and stared at the wall. It appeared that he and his Falcons were going to have to face the Melville Heights Bulldogs without the help of Joe Gunn in Saudi Arabia.

Nine

By the time the Falcons were in the dressing room changing into their game uniforms, Floyd did not know whether to thank his lucky stars or curse the fate that had befallen him.

The telephone scouting had gone well. The coaches who had faced the Melville Heights Bulldogs during the regular season were cooperative. They were helpful, too, with tips about what worked—and what didn't work—against the hard-running Bulldogs. Over and over again, their words confirmed what he had thought he was seeing—a weakness here, a strength there—when he watched them storm past the Williamstown Hornets last night.

The game plan fell into place easily. His Falcons were going to outrun the crazy-running Bulldogs. Floyd was sure they could do it. Jimmy, Gene, the twins—they all were fast. Even Eddie, for his size, was quick in getting down the court. Floyd was confident the Falcons could whip the Bulldogs at their own game. Beyond that, his team held a major weapon: Eddie, with his height, strength, and skill. If the Bulldogs had a serious weakness, it was at center. Their player was neither big enough nor quick enough to hinder Eddie. Eddie could beat him. On offense, he would be able to pour in points with his hook shots and rebounding. On defense, he would be able to out-muscle the other center on the boards and make sure the Bulldogs' shooters got only one shot.

In one way, even the Jimmy Gunn problem went well during the day. When the players returned from breakfast, Floyd caught his brother's eye. Eddie nodded slightly. So far, so good. Floyd got the same signal throughout the day, when he met the players at the Student Union for lunch, when they gathered at the field house for the campus tour and returned later, when they met for their light pregame dinner. Always, a slight nod from Eddie. And always from Floyd, a sigh of relief.

But in another way, the problem did not go well at all. At each turn during the day Jimmy seemed further and further removed from his teammates. There was nothing physical about his removal. He still stood and walked with them. He sat as close to them as ever during their meals. But increasingly Jimmy was not looking at the other members of the team, not seeing them, and they were not looking at him. He did not enter into the chatter. And nobody, not even Gene, invited him into it. They were like strangers to him. As for his teammates, they did not recognize Jimmy.

True, there had been no new explosion; Eddie's

slight nods at each meeting with Floyd confirmed that. But as the day wore on, these signals were less and less reassuring to him.

"Icicles are dangerous," Floyd's college coach once said. A cold feeling between players on a basketball team makes for errors—misplaced passes, fumbles, mental miscues. Although the Falcons had survived a lot of cold feeling during the season, they were never this cold, never this obvious. And, for sure, never in the face of such pressure—the best teams in the state playing in a do-or-die tournament. The icicles were forming.

At the team meeting late in the afternoon, Floyd tried to draw Jimmy and the others back together. Outlining the game plan, he emphasized the need for Jimmy and Gene to hurry downcourt in the wake of any turnover—Jimmy, the shooter, especially. "Be ready to take the ball and fire away," Floyd told him. "Eddie will be right behind you for the rebound if you miss."

Jimmy, without meeting Floyd's eyes, nodded his head.

"And you, Gene, I want you to shoot more often than usual. We're going to be running and gunning. The shooting has got to come from both sides, your side and Jimmy's. Both of you. Understand?"

Floyd's point was clear: Jimmy was the shooter. The Falcons always relied on his shooting. In a fast-break-style game, they would be counting even more heavily on those quick jump shots of his. Gene's occasional shots from the other side were sure to draw guarding strength away from Jimmy, helping him get free. Jimmy would be even more effective.

"Okay," Gene said flatly.

But none of it was working. No matter what Floyd said, Jimmy was not a member of the Cedar Grove Falcons basketball team. Not in his own eyes. Not in the eyes of his teammates. The long season of Jimmy Gunn, the boy from the big city, looking down on the faded uniforms, the cramped quarters, the different way of talking, the different haircuts, the farmer clothes—all of it had piled up beyond ignoring. The players had had enough. They had whipped Warren Tech. So who was Jimmy Gunn to look down on them? Well, he had done it one time too many. Unspoken, the others had decided not to take any more. They were freezing him out.

Even Gene, the easygoing redhead who had come closest to being friendly with Jimmy all through the season, was closing the door. The eruption the night before had drawn the line. The twin's sharp retort had spoken for all of them. Gene, whether he liked it or not, had to choose between Jimmy and the others. He was choosing his lifelong friends over the newcomer from the big city. He might not like making the choice, but there was no avoiding it.

Jimmy, glum and withdrawn, was thinking . . . who knew what? Floyd could not decipher the expression on his face. Perhaps he was angry or regretful. Or perhaps, worst of all, indifferent.

Floyd quickly shifted topics, launching into an explanation of Eddie's crucial role. "You're the real

84

key," he told Eddie. "You saw their center play last night. You can whip him, whip him bad. And you've got to do it. Be careful about fouling. We don't want him to do to you what you did to the big Warren Tech center. You know what I mean. But you've got to control the boards. The Bulldogs must get only one shot when they come running down the court. You've got to get the rebounds. We've got to get a second shot when we miss, and you've got to get the rebounds for us to do it. That's where we're going to win this game—on the boards. Okay?"

Eddie nodded. He understood.

But Floyd could not escape the feeling that nobody, Eddie included, was really listening.

For a moment he considered throwing out into the open the problem as he saw it. The wound might need lancing. Perhaps if he forced the players to discuss the problem they would be able to solve it. But Floyd considered the idea for only a brief moment. He did not want to rekindle the flames. Not now, anyway. Maybe later, if necessary. But for now, Floyd preferred the truce, uneasy as it was, to a crossfire of angry words.

Through it all—the telephone calls and strategic planning, the meals with the players, the team meeting—Floyd hoped for an interruption: a telephone call from Saudi Arabia.

The right words from Jimmy Gunn's father might —just might—thaw the deep freeze. Jimmy might hang up the telephone with a changed expression on his face. He might say the right words. And his teammates might—just might—see a change in Jimmy and offer him a new chance. Maybe, just maybe.

But, so far, there had been no telephone call from Saudi Arabia and as Floyd stood in the center of the dressing room and watched his players pull on their jerseys and tie their shoelaces, with time running out, he knew there was going to be no telephone call before the game.

The Falcons, with Eddie leading the way and Floyd bringing up the rear, walked down the corridor and onto the edge of the court. Floyd carried the large duffel bag full of towels for use on the bench.

Stepping into the glare of the arc lights, Floyd blinked. He could not resist a look to his right, where he and his players had slept the night before on tumbling mats. The floor glistened brightly.

The appearance of the Falcons brought the fans all around the arena to their feet with a roar, *"Fal-cons! Fal-cons!"*

The neutral fans who had adopted the underdog team in the faded uniforms against Warren Tech the night before were still pulling for them.

Floyd barely heard the cheers, but he recognized them and was grateful. He knew that in basketball, more than any other sport, cheering fans were an asset, actually worth points. With no more than a dozen people from Cedar Grove on hand, the Falcons needed the neutral fans on their side. Certainly, if the cheers could help, Floyd would accept them. He hoped that the twins, Gene, and Eddie heard the

cheers and understood that they were for Jimmy
Gunn, too. And he hoped that Jimmy heard them and
understood that the cheering fans had chosen the little team with the faded uniforms.

From the other end of the arena a stream of players
in black warm-up suits with gold trim jogged out of
the ramp onto the edge of the court, turned sharply,
and ran briskly toward their bench. The Melville
Heights Bulldogs had arrived.

Floyd walked up behind his players, now approaching their bench. With an effort, he put a grin
on his face. "We've got to work on our entrances," he
said.

Eddie, keeping his gaze downcourt, searching for
the center he was going to be facing, said, "It's what
happens after the entrance that counts."

Gene said, "Hey, yeah!"

Jimmy did not turn from staring at the Melville
Heights players pulling up to their bench. He did not
speak. They all had modish, over-the-ear haircuts.
Jimmy would have looked good in a black warm-up
suit with gold trim. Once again, Jimmy Gunn was
playing with the wrong bunch.

Floyd sent the players onto the court for their
warm-up shots and delivered his lineup to the
scorer's table. He stepped across and shook hands
with Jumbo Robbins, the Melville Heights coach.
Robbins, a huge man in both height and girth, had
become something of a legend in his ten years of
coaching the Bulldogs, not so much for his victories
but for his funny one-liners and his reputation for

87

giving entertaining speeches at athletic banquets. But he gave Floyd no one-liner jokes as they shook hands. He was serious and so was Floyd.

Heading back to his own bench, Floyd saw Gene's father approaching.

"We were late getting away," he said. "How's everything look?"

"Ready as we'll ever be," Floyd said.

"No trouble?"

Floyd glanced sideways at Wilson Montgomery. He sat down on the bench and Gene's father sat next to him.

"Gene called me at home this morning."

"Oh?"

"He said that things almost blew sky-high."

Mr. Montgomery, who had witnessed the shouting match between Jimmy Gunn and John Hartley in mid-season, was in a position to understand the seriousness of the eruption.

"I didn't know he called you," Floyd said.

"He was concerned."

Floyd managed a weak smile. "So was I," he said. Then he corrected himself. "So *am* I . . . still."

"No other trouble, though?"

"No other blowups. But things aren't good."

They sat together watching the Falcons move through their warm-up drills. Then Gene's father said, "There's talk around town about a caravan of the folks driving up tomorrow night." He paused. "If we're in the championship game," he added.

"We've got to win this one first," Floyd said, not

taking his eyes off the Falcons on the court.

"Sure."

Floyd looked at Gene's father. He had been a big help to Floyd all through the long season. He truly deserved the title Floyd had jokingly bestowed, honorary assistant coach. He started to ask a question: "Are they sure they wouldn't be embarrassed—I mean, if they came up in a caravan to watch us play?" But he did not speak.

Gene's father seemed to hear the question anyway. He placed a hand on Floyd's shoulder. "Everyone in Cedar Grove is mighty proud of you and the boys," he said. "Even Big John. He won't admit it, but I could tell."

Floyd recalled the night before when he sat on a tumbling mat, wrapped in a gray-and-green blanket, staring into the gloom, and guessed at Big John's remarks over coffee at the window table. He remembered the half dream in the middle of the night—Big John frowning, just sitting there and frowning.

"He may surprise you," Mr. Montgomery said with a knowing twinkle in his eye. "He just may."

Floyd started to ask what he meant, but there was no time. The players were returning to the bench.

"We've got to win this one first," Floyd said again, getting to his feet to greet the players.

Gene's father called out, "Good luck," and walked away, heading for his seat in the stands.

Ten

Floyd extended his hands into the circle of players, clasping hands.

"Same hoops as last night. No higher off the floor, no smaller—just as easy to put the ball in."

He watched the players' faces as he spoke, trying to read their minds. He needed to know the right words to say.

Jimmy's look of arrogance was gone. In its place he wore a sullen expression. He looked lonely. Floyd felt sorry for him at this moment before the tip-off. Jimmy had spent the season setting the stage for his troubles. Now, finally, one of the players had snapped back at him, and in the following twenty-four hours his teammates, all of them, had silently lined up against him, and he knew it. He was alone. What was there for Floyd to say?

Gene had the look of combat in his eye. At this moment, the troubles of the last twenty-four hours seemed far away and behind him. He was ready to play. That was good. Eddie's jaw was taut, a signal of readiness that Floyd had seen for years. Eddie's mind was on the game. That was good. The twins, unblinking, revealed nothing. Floyd wondered again which of them had barked at Jimmy, but it didn't matter. For now he would settle for their blank stares.

The clasped hands in the center of the circle pumped three times.

"Get 'em," Floyd said.

The players broke the circle, and the starters—Jimmy and Gene, Eddie, the twins—headed onto the court.

Floyd, taking a long step, reached out and slapped Jimmy on the rear end. "Go, shooter!" he said. Jimmy did not turn around. Floyd backed up and sat down on the bench next to his three substitutes.

The referee was walking toward the center circle with the ball in his hands.

All around the arena, everyone was standing. The fans in black and gold, all in a group, were shouting and waving pennants. But their cheers were drowned out by the roar from every other corner of the arena—*"Fal-cons! Fal-cons!"*

Eddie and the Bulldogs' center crouched for the leap. The referee between them sent the ball spinning into the air and stepped back. The two centers released their springs. They went up.

Eddie outjumped the Melville Heights center by an easy three inches. He flicked the ball to Gene, and Gene, without taking a step, fired a hard overhand pass half the length of the court. Jimmy, racing for the corner, brought in the ball. He dribbled once. He jumped. He fired. And—*swish!*—he scored.

The huge scoreboards blinked: Falcons 2, Bulldogs 0.

At the bench, Floyd gave an involuntary nod of approval. He liked the beginning—a quick strike for a score. The Falcons had set the pace in the first play of the game. With it, they had announced their plan. They were going to outrun the running Bulldogs. And with perfect execution they had scored. But Floyd did not stand and cheer. He did not shoot a fist into the air. He remained seated. He was waiting for the test to come. The Falcons had to stop the hard-running Bulldogs.

Eddie pummeled Jimmy with a congratulatory slap on the back as the Falcons began retreating into their defensive positions. Jimmy gave a small smile.

The Melville Heights guards brought the ball up the court. They were not the match of the Warren Tech guards from the night before. They were neither dazzling dribblers nor ball-handling magicians. But they were quick and clever. They got the ball across the center stripe in short order. Roy and Ray moved out against them warily.

Eddie raced to the lane in front of the basket with the Melville Heights center, flanked by Jimmy and Gene.

The Melville Heights guard shot a two-handed pass down the sideline to a forward. The forward instantly bounced the ball in to the center under the basket.

Eddie, outside of him, swarmed over the center. He was sure to block the shot when the center started his move upward. But the center did not go up. He let the ball trail off his fingertips in a soft bounce pass under the basket. Out of nowhere, one of the guards zipped through. He picked off the ball and, hardly seeming to touch it, sent it twirling up toward the basket. Eddie, caught behind the center, had no chance to block the shot. Jimmy and Gene, coming in, were too late. The ball rolled over the rim and dropped through.

Floyd was on his feet now. Eddie had been tricked. The Bulldogs, well coached, had fooled him. They were using his very strength under the boards as a weapon against him. Instead of sending their shorter, weaker center into a futile one-on-one battle with Eddie, they were using him as a foil to hold Eddie's attention. That way, another player could race through for a shot.

Floyd, waving his arms and trying to shout above the roar of the crowd, caught Eddie's attention as he ran down the court to take up his offensive position. With his eyes, Floyd asked the question. Eddie saw Floyd and understood the question. He nodded the answer. Yes, he knew what had happened to him. And, yes, he would make his play differently next time. Floyd sat back down on the bench as the twins brought the ball back into play.

From there the two teams traded field goals at the end of each wild sortie up and down the court. The running Falcons and the running Bulldogs matched each other point for point. Eddie's superiority in rebounding got the Falcons a second, sometimes even a third, try at the goal when a teammate's shot missed. But at the other end of the court, the Bulldogs' forwards were hot from fifteen feet out. Their swishers nullified Eddie's dominance of the backboard. He had no rebounds to grab. One shot was enough for the hot-handed Bulldogs.

The hot shooting of the Bulldogs' forwards bothered Floyd less than the gnawing feeling that his Falcons were off their game. Something was wrong. Something small, barely discernable, but dangerous. True, the Falcons were keeping pace with the Bulldogs on the scoreboard. Jimmy, Gene, and Eddie all were shooting well. The Bulldogs tried the pass to the center for a drop-off to a guard once more, but only once. Eddie saw the play developing and took the ball out of the center's hands. As for the accurate gunning of the Bulldogs' forwards, Floyd was satisfied for the moment that the Falcons' tenacious defense would shut them down. That failing, there were tactical changes he could order. The Bulldogs' early streak of hot shooting was not worrisome—yet.

But a deep frown creased Floyd's forehead as he leaned forward on the bench, elbows on knees, and stared at the action on the court.

The twins were bringing the ball up the court following the Bulldogs' latest field goal from the edge of the keyhole.

The score was 16–14, with the Bulldogs in the lead. The clock showed less than a minute to go in the first quarter.

Jimmy moved out to meet the twin dribbling toward the center stripe. It was the right move for him, but there was something tentative about Jimmy's movements. Floyd had noticed this unsureness before. It was as if he did not expect to receive the ball from the twin. The Melville Heights player guarding Jimmy sensed his uncertainty and relaxed. Good players faked the maneuver to lull their guards into a momentary lapse so they could get themselves open for a pass. Jimmy himself was adept at the trick. But this was no fake. Floyd knew each of his players well enough to tell the difference between acting and the real thing. This was the real thing.

Either way, Jimmy was open for a pass.

The twin dribbled over the center stripe and sent a pass across the court to his brother.

Floyd's frown deepened. The pass should have gone to Jimmy, whether he was expecting it or not. A pass to Jimmy, a quick jump shot, a score—that was the game plan. But instead, the Falcons were still far to the outside with a guard holding the ball near the center stripe.

The twin passed down the sideline to Gene. Gene drove for the basket. Eddie pivoted, blocking the Bulldogs' center. Gene dribbled under the basket. He flicked the ball upward with his right hand. The ball teetered on the rim and dropped off. The Bulldogs' center tried to step around Eddie, but Eddie stayed in front of him. Then he leaped and tipped the ball back up toward the basket. The ball bounced off the backboard and dropped through.

The fans cheering the Falcons were on their feet with a roar.

But Floyd at the bench did not move. His frown remained in place. The Falcons were not freezing Jimmy out. He had scored six of their sixteen points on a pair of jump shots and a driving lay-up. He had taken two other shots that missed. He was getting the ball. But he was not expecting to get it. He was expecting a freeze-out. The signs were all there. If Jimmy continued to expect a freeze-out, he was sure to get it. Maybe it already had started. The twin, recognizing Jimmy's tentative move, had sent the ball across the court to his brother. It was the wrong play.

If the Falcons hoped to outshoot the fast-breaking Bulldogs, they needed Jimmy Gunn's deadly jump shots from the corner to do it. It had been the same all season. Eddie was important. Gene was important. The twins were important. But in the final analysis, Jimmy's shooting made the difference. If he did not get the ball, he could not shoot. And if he did not shoot, the Falcons were headed for trouble.

The Bulldogs, with the last seconds of the quarter ticking away, raced wildly down the court. A guard, taking the pass inbounds, wound up like a baseball pitcher and fired an overhand pass the length of the court.

The Falcons, backpedaling, turned and ran full speed.

Looking over his shoulder, Eddie veered toward the ball. A Bulldog forward coming across went for the ball. Eddie arrived with him. They somehow avoided a collision. A hand hit the ball. Then another hand slapped it. Other players were rushing in. The ball bounced out of bounds.

The referee's swinging arm gave the signal: Falcons' ball.

Floyd stood. The quarter was almost at an end. Time for one quick play.

Roy took the ball out of bounds. In front of him, players darted everywhere. Roy stared impassively at the running figures for a moment, holding the ball in his right hand. Then he spotted Gene near the center circle, cutting sharply to his right and breaking free. Roy passed to Gene.

Gene took in the ball. He turned and looked down the court. The final seconds were ticking away. Jimmy, in the corner, was breaking away from his guard. He was free. Gene looked at him, then he looked away.

Floyd flinched.

Gene looked at Eddie racing for a spot under the basket. The Bulldogs' center was in hot pursuit. Eddie was a risky target. Gene turned back to Jimmy and sent a two-handed rifle shot toward him. But it was too late. The Bulldogs' guard had recovered and Jimmy's moment of freedom had passed. The Bulldog player lunged and got a piece of the ball. It skittered crazily back toward the center of the court. Jimmy and the Melville Heights guard dived for the ball. Gene rushed forward to enter the melee.

They were still scrapping for the loose ball when the buzzer sounded, ending the first quarter.

The scoreboard showed: Falcons 16, Bulldogs 16.

Eleven

Floyd stood up, hitched up his slacks, ran a hand
through his hair, and waited at the sideline for his
players. As they passed him one at a time, heading for
the duffel bag full of towels, Floyd watched their
faces and made up his mind what he was going to say.
More importantly, he decided how he was going to
say it.

The players, mopping the perspiration off their
faces, gathered in a semicircle in front of him.

On the court, cheerleaders were taking the crowd
of sixteen thousand fans through a deafening sequence of shouts.

The players leaned in, cocking their heads to be
sure they heard Floyd's words above the roar.

Floyd thought, You'll be able to hear me, all right.

"What kind of a game do you think you're playing?" he snapped.

Floyd surprised even himself. He was fairly bark-
ing, and Floyd Bentley never barked at his players.

The words dripped with sarcasm. Floyd Bentley never used sarcasm with his players. He sounded angry, but Floyd Bentley never got angry with his players.

Around him, eyes widened.

Floyd turned to Gene with a glare. "You, Gene, you stood out there in the center circle trying to make up your mind what to do with the ball, and while you stood there wondering what to do, the Bulldogs were moving in. Your hesitation cost us a possible field goal. Where have you been all season?"

Gene's eyes widened another notch. He was startled by the sharpness of the rebuke. He opened his mouth to speak. Then he closed it again.

Floyd looked at Roy. "When you're bringing the ball down the court, your job is to get the ball into the hands of somebody in a position to score"—he waggled a forefinger in Roy's face—"and not to play catch with your brother out around the center stripe. In that last drive of ours, you had Jimmy open—free right in front of you—and you sent the ball over to Ray instead of firing it into scoring range. Weren't you at the meeting when we discussed the game plan? Or don't you know what outrunning a team means?"

Roy blinked at the harsh words, but said nothing.

Floyd looked at the faces around him. Their expressions were changing. The looks of astonishment were fading. The eyes were narrowing. The jaws were clenched. The surprise was turning to anger. Good, good, Floyd thought. If they wanted to be angry, better they be angry with the coach—all of them together—than angry with each other. Much, much better.

It was Eddie's turn. If Floyd was going to dish out tough talk, some of it had to go to his brother. "Are you getting lazy out there already?" he asked.

"Huh?"

Floyd ignored Eddie's startled response. "You've got their center whipped," he went on. "But he's still in there trying. And if you lay down, he'll run over you. A couple of times out there you were toying with him when you should have been working on him." He paused. "If you let him whip you even once, you may be giving up the points we need to win."

Floyd thought for a moment that he read in Eddie's eyes an understanding of his snapping at the players. But, no, Eddie had been taken by surprise, and now he was getting angry, same as the others.

"Don't let up," Floyd finished.

Eddie said nothing. He stared at Floyd and nodded.

Floyd turned to Jimmy. Jimmy was watching Floyd closely. He seemed to be expecting what was coming, knowing already what the words were going to be. He was waiting. Floyd needed to deliver a shock, more so with Jimmy than any of the others, a jolt to bring him back to life and into the game. And then he needed silence, absolute silence, from Jimmy. A nod maybe, but no words.

"You're moving around out there like a zombie," Floyd said. "I've seen faster movement in the line at the post office." He paused. "Are you dead?"

Floyd and Jimmy stared into each other's eyes. The silence between them seemed to be encased in the semicircle of players, blocking out the roar of the fans' cheers rolling down on them from all sides. Nobody said anything. Not Floyd. Not Jimmy. Not anyone.

Jimmy had never heard this kind of talk from Floyd. None of them had, not even Eddie. Floyd did not nag his players. He did not insult them or needle them with jibes. He did not embarrass them. He preferred cool logic to histrionics. He treated his players as sensible people able to understand good reasoning. But Floyd had never before faced such uncertainty, such tentativeness, in his Falcons. He had to shock them, all of them. He had to jerk them back from their troubles and their doubts, to return them to the game. He had to do it or the Bulldogs were going to whip the Falcons. And he had only the brief intermission to do it in.

In the silence—a moment? a minute? an hour?—Floyd counted the reactions he might get from Jimmy. There might be a sneer or an arrogant shrug of the shoulders. Perhaps a cutting remark. Two weeks ago, those reactions—one or more of them—were almost a certainty. But now the Falcons had turned on Jimmy, one of them with loud anger, the others with a silence no less clear in its meaning. The Cedar Grove boys had had all they were taking from the big-city boy. Was Jimmy's answer still going to be a sneer, an arrogant shrug, a smart remark?

Or, Floyd wondered, might Jimmy's reaction be

102

even worse. He might turn on his heel, leave the court, quit the game here and now. Floyd knew the risk. He had weighed the chances. Now he had made his bet.

Finally, Jimmy nodded slightly, still not speaking.

Floyd took a deep breath. "Okay," he said, his voice returning to the tone of the persuading instructor. "Now, quickly, about those hot-shooting forwards. There's a way to cool them off. We need to extend the zone defense out a step or two, just a step or two. So far, they've been picking their spots for their shots. They've been standing where they want to stand. We've got to end that. Back them up a step or two. You stand where they want to stand for their shots. It'll knock them off stride, not much maybe, but a little, and that will be enough. They'll start missing. And when they miss a few, they'll start trying to drive around you." Floyd managed a grin. "And that's when you take the ball away from them."

The intermission was ending. The players clasped hands with Floyd, pumped three times, and turned toward the court. There were no smiles among them.

Floyd sent up a silent prayer that his sideline tactics had been for the best.

The twins, Jimmy, and Gene managed to shove back the firing line of the Bulldogs' forwards to an uncomfortable range, but they still were hitting more often than they were missing. Floyd could not help admiring their skill. At least they were no longer pumping in shots with the automatic accuracy of the

103

first quarter. They were missing some of them, and each miss, Floyd knew, gave rise to a hint of doubt. The hints of doubt were sure to build up in their minds. For a shooter, when doubt came in, accuracy went out. As the second quarter ticked away, they were missing even more of their shots. Then, as Floyd had predicted, they started trying to drive around Jimmy and Gene. They wanted to go in for lay-ups. They wanted to force the Falcons' zone defense back a step or two. But with Eddie moving out to help Jimmy and Gene, the Falcons tied them in knots.

Increasingly, Eddie was wearing down the Bulldogs' center under the basket. He outjumped, outfought, and outreached him at every turn. Twice, stepping out toward the free-throw line, Eddie simply left the confused Bulldogs' center behind, and scored on fifteen-foot jump shots.

Midway through the quarter, Floyd began sending William Logan into the game—first for Gene, then Jimmy, then Eddie. If the furious pace was to continue, the players in the front line needed an occasional breather.

William's play caused Floyd to raise an eyebrow. William, a junior, was a substitute on a small Class B team, playing against the frontline players of one of the best Class A teams in the state. But whether working at forward in place of Jimmy or Gene, or substituting for Eddie at center, William displayed remarkable skill and poise, more than Floyd had seen during the regular season. It was as if William were the better for the tougher competition. Once he stepped up and stole the ball out of a forward's hands. The fans roared their approval of the gangly William in his faded uniform against the sleek city boy in a uniform of brilliant black and gold. William, coming out of the tussle with the ball in his hands, hardly seemed to notice. Straight-faced, he turned and passed the ball downcourt.

Through it all, Floyd remained on the bench, now leaning forward, now sitting back with legs crossed. He was watching more for signs of trouble than signs of triumph and he thought he saw them. A twin passing to Jimmy seemed by the very manner of his throw to say, "So, there!" Jimmy, when shooting, was pressing too hard, and missing more than he hit. Fortunately, Eddie was there for the rebound. Whether a hit or a miss, Jimmy's face feigned indifference. Floyd saw it. So did the players. Gene, appearing angered, shouted, "C'mon!" at him once. If Jimmy heard him, he did not show it.

But the Falcons were working hard, and they had the lead to show for it. At the halftime buzzer, Floyd stood up and looked at the scoreboard: 32–28.

Twelve

Walking off the court and heading for the corridor leading to the dressing room, Floyd fell in step with Eddie. "You've got that center of theirs wondering which county he's in," Floyd said. "We'll be feeding you the ball a lot in the second half. Poke it in there."

Eddie nodded. Then he turned to Floyd. "What was all that business at the end of the first quarter?"

"You know what that business was."

"You made everyone mad."

Floyd grinned slightly. "Yeah, I know," he said.

"I thought for a minute that Jimmy was going to blow us all apart because of what you were saying to him."

"Well, he didn't," Floyd said. Then he asked, "Do you think anyone noticed that he didn't blow us all apart?"

"I don't know," Eddie said, turning into the dressing room.

Floyd, following him, said, "It's going to be all

right." But he had his fingers crossed in his pocket as he spoke. Then, to the players scattered around the dressing room, he called out, "Just relax for a minute. Just relax."

While the players slumped on benches, breathing heavily, Floyd moved among them. He had different words for each. He told the twins, "When you're bringing the ball upcourt, cut loose with a long pass once in a while. We want to keep 'em running." And, "Take a few shots from the outside. It'll keep their defense from closing in on Eddie." To Jimmy, he said, "Too many bad shots. You know it as well as I do. Take a shot when you've got it, but don't force it." To Gene: "Keep driving for the basket. You've got that side of their zone whipped." And he congratulated William, "Beautiful, beautiful. You're doing great."

He did not mention the twin's suspect pass to Jimmy, Gene's angry shout, or Jimmy's act of indifference after a shot. And, above all, he did not refer to his harangue at the end of the first quarter.

"A couple of things, now," Floyd said when he finished his round of individual talks with his players. The halftime intermission was running out. Looking at the faces around him, he wished again he could read their minds. If they held together, they could win, no doubt. If they fell apart, they were doomed to lose for sure. One word, one scowl, one "heavy ball" pass—anything might spark disaster for the Falcons.

The players watched Floyd, giving no clue to what was going through their minds.

"Get the ball to Eddie as much as you can," Floyd

continued. "Eddie owns that Melville Heights center. Let's collect on it." Eddie nodded unconsciously. "And, don't slow down, don't let up. Keep running. We're beating them by carrying the game—their own style of game—right to them, and jamming it down their throats. That's the way we're going to win. This is no time to let them gain control. So keep running."

The players trooped out of the dressing room and headed for the court for their warm-up shots. Floyd followed them down the corridor.

At the bench, his eye wandered past the scorer's table. For a brief second his gaze met that of the Melville Heights coach. Floyd saw the same expression he had seen on the face of the Warren Tech coach the night before. The message was clear. His team was losing to the team from—where?—Cedar Grove, and there was nothing he could do about it. Four of the five Falcons had played together all their lives, so the Bulldogs, a disparate bunch who entered high school from several different junior high schools, could not hope to match them in teamwork. Jumbo Robbins needed a miracle, and he did not see one on the horizon. Only Floyd knew how dangerously close the Falcons were coming to providing the miracle the Bulldogs needed. If the rift between Jimmy and the others widened a bit more, the Falcons' teamwork would unravel and give Jumbo Robbins the break his team needed.

Floyd took a deep breath and turned his attention to his players on the court. He watched them until they returned to the bench for the final seconds before the start of the second half.

In the circle at the bench Floyd and the players clasped hands. "Remember," he said above the din of the crowd, "this game isn't over yet."

But it was.

Floyd sensed in the opening minutes of the second half that his Falcons were on top and determined to stay there. The players seemed to sense it, too. So did the Bulldogs.

True, the signs of trouble were still evident. Jimmy, unsmiling, appearing indifferent, seemed apart from the others despite his steady flow of field goals. Gene did not shout at him again, but it was clear on several occasions that he came close to it. The twins, in a way, ignored Jimmy. They still passed to him. They interacted with him. But they were looking through him more than at him when they exchanged the ball.

Floyd was hoping the signs of trouble would diminish with each step the Falcons took toward victory. But it didn't happen. He decided he would settle for what he had—a team that wanted to win, and was able to win, in spite of all the troubles.

Eddie was the complete master of the Melville Heights center. He pumped in sixteen points in the second half and swept the boards time and again. Jimmy, taking more care with his shots from the corner, added ten points. Roy and Ray, shooting from the outside, each got a field goal. Gene, although he did not score in the second half, set up a half-dozen field goals with passes to Eddie and Jimmy.

The final seconds of the game—with the crowd counting off the seconds, *ten, nine, eight*—seemed almost to catch the Falcons by surprise. They had been running at top speed. They had been shooting, jumping, reaching. And then, as if without notice, the game was at an end.

All around the arena the crowd roared, *"Fal-cons! Fal-cons!"* But on the court the players, winded and worn out, just stood for a moment. Nobody shouted or clapped anyone on the back. Nobody leaped into the air. Nobody even smiled. They just stood there.

Floyd stepped onto the court and found himself facing Jumbo Robbins. They shook hands. Robbins said something, but Floyd did not catch the words above the roar of the crowd. It didn't matter. Floyd acknowledged the remark with a nod and turned to his players, now walking off the court.

Floyd quietly shook each player's hand as the team walked past him on the way to the dressing room. Then he followed the last one, one of the twins, toward the ramp.

The huge scoreboards at either end of the arena read: Falcons 66, Bulldogs 52. The team from Cedar Grove was in the championship game.

"If," Floyd sighed to himself, "we've still got a team tomorrow night."

"Quiet! Quiet!"

Floyd was shouting above the noise in the dressing room. His players had realized that the game was over, they had won, and they were heading for the championship game. The celebration had started when the first player, Gene, entered the dressing room. Then everyone coming into the room joined in.

Everybody seemed to be screaming something. Gene, as usual, was leading the cheers, shooting a fist into the air with each shout. Eddie, normally restrained in his dual role of coach's brother and the only senior on the starting five, was cutting loose with uncharacteristic whoops. Even Jimmy had a smile on his face as he watched his teammates unwind in jubilation. The twins grinned and one of them gave a shout. William, with a wide grin, moved around the room, giving everyone a slap on the shoulder.

"Quiet a minute!" Floyd shouted.

He waited for the cheering to die down. He watched the faces around him and marveled at the therapeutic value of victory. Angry, disgruntled, unhappy—the expressions turned into grins, laughter, and shouts in the glorious wash of victory. Grudges were laid aside. Old slights were forgotten. Bitterness went back beneath the surface. All was beautiful—for the moment, at least. Floyd had seen it happen time and again during the season. He wondered if the medicine of victory would work one more time for a team of Cedar Grove boys and a boy from a big school on the outskirts of Houston.

There was a knock at the dressing room door, but Floyd ignored it.

The room began to quiet down.

"Tomorrow night," Floyd said, then he stopped. The words were coming hard. "Tomorrow night we play for the championship."

Everyone gave out with a roaring cheer. Floyd held out his hands, signaling for quiet. "The championship of the Class A division," he said.

Another cheer rocked the room.

Floyd waited for quiet, then waited another moment. Finally he said softly, "I am very proud of you." After another moment he turned to the twin near the door and said, "Okay, open the door."

The stream of people pushing and shoving their way through the door was even larger than the crowd of the night before. Floyd spotted an occasional familiar face—Gene Montgomery's parents, his own father and mother, other parents of the players—and recognized a couple of reporters from the night before. But the strangers outnumbered the familiar faces by an easy ten to one.

Relatives gravitated toward the players. The twins were getting hugs from their parents. William Logan's father, beaming with pride at his son's role in the victory, surveyed the wild scene with a look of wonder on his face. Jimmy's mother turned from her son and quietly asked Floyd, "Did you reach Joe?"

"No. He was out at the construction site. I left a message. Maybe he will call before tomorrow night's game."

"I'm sure he will," she said and, without pressing Floyd for his reasons, moved back into the crowd toward Jimmy.

Floyd used both hands to accept the congratulatory handshakes of the strangers coming at him, seemingly by the dozens. Reporters shouted questions at him. He tried to answer. He saw a television cameraman attempting to elbow his way through. All of it—the crowd, the strange faces, the shouting, the shoving—seemed unreal.

Then the crowd began to thin out almost as quickly as it had entered. The well-wishers had had their handshakes. They were on their way back to their seats to watch the second game—the clash to determine the Falcons' opponent in the championship game. The reporters had gotten the quotes they needed and were returning to the press box. The smattering of Cedar Grove people were heading for their cars and the long drive home. A couple of the players let out a final whoop of victory as the door closed.

Don Benson appeared in front of Floyd. "Well, once again, congratulations, Coach Bentley." He turned to the players. "Congratulations to all of you. You deserved to win. You played well."

"Thank you," Floyd said.

"I have rooms for you tonight," Benson said. "A lot of the Warren Tech folks had rooms for all three nights of the tournament but checked out and went home today, as I thought they would."

"Oh, I . . ." Floyd said, and stopped. He had not given one thought to accommodations during the busy and worrisome day. "That's—"

"I think we ought to sleep on the court again," one of the twins interrupted.

113

He looked at Jimmy as he spoke.

By his number, Floyd identified him: Roy.

Others turned and looked at Jimmy.

Jimmy glared at Roy a moment. Then, with darting eyes, he looked at the other players. He said nothing.

"Yeah," Gene said. "Yeah, it was good enough for us last night, and it's good enough for us tonight."

Floyd looked at Gene. He wondered if the easygoing redhead knew he was adding to a jab at Jimmy.

"I think so, too," Eddie said. "It was good luck for us last night."

Floyd grabbed at the straw his brother offered. "Yeah, it sure was," he said. "What do the rest of you think?"

Somebody said, "Yeah." Others nodded. Jimmy said nothing. He did not move.

"I guess it's unanimous," Floyd said. He turned to Benson. "Is it okay?"

"You really want to?" asked the unbelieving Benson.

Floyd grinned. "It seems unanimous," he repeated.

Benson laughed. "You boys from Cedar Grove really carry things a bit far when it comes to feeling at home on a basketball court, don't you?"

"Will it be all right?"

"I'm sure it will," Benson said. "I'll arrange things."

Thirteen

"I'm going home."

Jimmy had come out of the shower room only seconds after entering, toweling himself as he walked. Now he was throwing on his clothes as fast as his hands could move.

He spoke the words in a low, conversational tone.

Floyd, seated on the training table, stared at him in disbelief. "Home?" he said.

"Yes, home. You know—going, leaving, quitting. Understand?"

Floyd shot a glance at the shower-room door. The others were still inside. He heard a couple of whoops and laughs—Gene's voice, then Eddie's—above the gushing sound of the water. Jimmy had not told the players of his intentions—that much was certain. If they knew, Eddie, and maybe Gene, would have followed him out of the shower—to argue, to try to dissuade, something. The others for sure did not hear

Jimmy's softly spoken declaration above the noise of the water and their own shouts.

Floyd had only a minute, maybe two, before the rest of the players started coming out of the shower room.

"Let's talk a minute," he said.

"Nothing to talk about," Jimmy answered. He was stuffing in his shirttail and buckling his belt. "I'm going. I've had it. I've had enough."

"Was something said in the shower room?"

"Nope."

"Well then, what?"

Jimmy ran a comb through his hair carelessly. "My mother and grandparents are waiting, and—"

"Do they know what you're intending to do?"

"No, but they'll find out. They're waiting to say good-bye before leaving. I'm leaving with them."

Floyd's mind raced through a dizzying sequence of scenes. He was trying to find the right words, to decide on the right move. But every idea seemed blocked by a picture from the past. He saw the angry face of the twin who had shouted at Jimmy. If Floyd had made room reservations, as he should have, the explosion never would have occurred. He saw himself seated at a desk, telephone in hand, leaving a message for Jimmy's father. If he had called earlier, all might have been smoothed over by now. He saw Jimmy's face, eyes darting around the room like those of a trapped animal, at the moment Roy suggested sleeping on tumbling mats a second night. Again, if he had made room reservations in the first place, the scene

116

never would have occurred. He saw, too, the sneers, the arrogant shrugs of the long season, each a sign of trouble brewing. If Floyd had attacked the problem the first time it had popped up—or the second or the third time—maybe tonight there would be no problem. But he hadn't.

Now he had to wipe out months of the lingering troubles in one stroke.

But why? Why not let the snooty, big-city boy quit, walk out, go home? True, he'd scored a lot of points for the Falcons. But he'd made trouble for everybody, even for himself. Let William Logan play in his place. Win the championship without Jimmy. Why not?

Because the Falcons needed Jimmy if they were to have a chance of winning? Because Floyd Bentley, the first-year coach, needed to keep his scoring star from walking out to avoid not only defeat but the label of failure as a coach? Floyd let the reasons race through his mind. They were good ones. But they were not the real reasons why he had to stop Jimmy from quitting. The real reason that Jimmy Gunn had to stay and play in the championship game with the Falcons was in plain fact the future well-being of Jimmy Gunn. Jimmy must not make this mistake. He had a long life ahead of him, and he must not carry the brand of quitter—not in his own eyes, not in the eyes of family, teammates, schoolmates. He had to be talked out of his decision.

Floyd hopped off the training table, glancing again at the door to the shower room. The players were going to be coming out any second. He turned to Jimmy. "C'mon," he said. He snapped the word out. It was not an invitation. It was not a suggestion. It was a command.

Jimmy blinked at him.

"You can afford to give me two minutes," Floyd said. "I've put up with your mouth all season long. You can put up with mine for two minutes. You owe me that much."

Floyd did not wait for an answer. He walked to the shower-room door, stuck his head into the steamy room, and shouted, "Hey! I'll be back in a minute. I'm going out with Jimmy to see his folks."

Again he did not wait for an answer. He turned and walked to the dressing-room door and opened it. "Let's go," he said. "You're going to have to listen to me. No way out."

Jimmy shrugged and walked through the door.

"This way," Floyd said. "To the office. We can talk there."

They turned and headed down the corridor, picking their way through the fans milling toward the ramps that led to the seats for the second game.

Wilson Montgomery suddenly materialized in front of them.

"We're hitting the road for home, and I—" He stopped in midsentence. Glancing at Jimmy, then back at Floyd, his eyes asked a question. But he did not speak it. Instead, he said, "I'll be back in the morning."

"In the morning?"

"Sure," he said. "It's Saturday. The store can do without me."

Floyd smiled at the Falcons' honorary assistant coach. Gene's father knew that Floyd needed time alone, away from the players, to gather information and develop a game plan. He also knew the dangers of leaving the troubled players untended. He would be on hand to help.

"Thanks," Floyd said.

"I'll stick my head in and say good night to Gene, and we'll be on our way."

"Tell Jimmy's folks that he'll be right there. They're expecting him."

"Sure," he said, and disappeared into the crowd.

Floyd and Jimmy walked to the door of the office. Floyd tapped lightly on the door and, getting no response, opened it. The room was empty. They went inside. Floyd closed the door. He gestured to the chair at the desk and Jimmy sat down. Floyd took a seat on a chair against the wall.

Jimmy wore an expression of exasperation, patience wearing thin in a boring exercise. "Before you walk out," Floyd said, "you're going to think for a few minutes about what you're doing, and you're going to decide that this idea was a mistake—a mistake you don't want to make—and then you're not going to walk out after all, and you and I will be the only ones who ever know you even thought about it."

Jimmy took a deep breath. "The whole thing has

been a mistake. I never should have come out for basketball in the first place. I didn't want to do it. My father talked me into it."

"Your father wanted what was best for you."

Floyd's statement, spoken in a flat, matter-of-fact tone, seemed to derail Jimmy's line of thought. Jimmy turned his head and stared at the floor in silence a moment. Floyd unconsciously glanced at the telephone on the desk. He wished again he had tried earlier to reach Jimmy's father. Jimmy Gunn would listen to his father. A telephone conversation might have—probably would have—forestalled Jimmy's decision to walk out. A telephone conversation might yet solve the problem—if Floyd could keep Jimmy from going home with his family and leaving the championship game behind.

"You know that's true, don't you—that your father wants what is best for you?" Floyd asked.

Jimmy looked at Floyd. "He doesn't know . . ."

"Doesn't know what?"

"This bunch is not for me, everybody so buddy-buddy, and everybody related to somebody else, and . . ." He shrugged and let the words trail off as if the explanation were obvious.

"They're different from you, huh?"

Jimmy snorted. His lips curled in a half smile. "Boy, you can say that again."

"And you're different from them."

"Huh?"

"I said, and you're different from them."

"I hope so."

"Was everyone alike at that school in Houston?" Floyd asked. "I find that hard to imagine."

"Well, no . . ."

"There were some people who were different from you?"

"Sure."

"And you were different from some of the people there? Even some of the people on the basketball team, huh?"

"Yeah, sure."

"It's exactly the same at Cedar Grove High. Gene is different. Eddie is different. The twins"—Floyd smiled—"are alike, but the two of them are different from the others." He paused. "And you're different. So what?"

"You don't understand."

"Then explain it to me."

"Well, the Warren Tech team, and then the Melville Heights team . . ."

"Your kind of team, huh? Large squads. Fancy uniforms. Lots of coaches. Your kind of outfit, huh, instead of the Falcons—small squad, faded uniforms, and one coach who's green as grass?"

"I didn't mean . . ."

"Sure you did."

Jimmy opened his mouth to protest, but he didn't speak. He closed his mouth.

"It was written all over your face out there on the court," Floyd said. "I saw it. The other players saw it."

Jimmy shrugged.

For a moment they were silent. Floyd leaned back in his chair. He tried to appear relaxed. This was the moment to change Jimmy's mind. Floyd sensed it. He sensed, too, that the moment would be fleeting. He had to say the words, and he had to have the right ones.

He spoke softly. "You're not going to walk out on the team," he said. "You're not going to tell them that you're a quitter. You're not going to tell your mother and your grandparents that you are a quitter. You're not going to tell your father that you were a quitter. And most important of all, you're not going to live the rest of your life telling yourself that you were a quitter."

Jimmy stared at the floor. He nibbled his lower lip absently. Briefly, a frown creased his forehead, then vanished.

Floyd watched him. "You're going to stay. You're going to play. And you and I will always know—most importantly, *you* will always know—that you made the right decision at a critical juncture in your life."

Jimmy looked up at Floyd. He nodded slightly.

"Good," Floyd said, standing up. "Let's go."

The players were finishing dressing when Floyd and Jimmy walked in the dressing room. A muffled roar from the crowd above them signaled that the second game was under way and somebody had scored.

"We going to watch them?" Eddie asked.

"Yeah," Floyd said. "It's our bedroom, isn't it?"

122

Fourteen

"Coach." The voice was a husky whisper. "Coach."

Floyd, asleep on a tumbling mat beneath a gray-and-green blanket, heard the voice somewhere in the back of his mind. Then he felt a gentle nudging of his shoulder. He raised his head with a start.

"Huh?" he said groggily.

The arena was gray with the first light of morning. There was a slight chill in the air. Floyd saw the outline of a man bending over him. The man was wearing a baseball cap and a light Windbreaker jacket.

"I'm the night watchman, coach." The man still held his voice to a whisper. "You've got a telephone call in the office . . . from Saudi Arabia . . . and I thought I ought to wake you for it. Might be important."

"Uh-huh," Floyd mumbled. He lifted himself into a sitting position. "Right. Sure. Be right there." He rubbed his eyes. "What time is it?"

"Few minutes after six."

"Okay. Thanks. Tell them I'll be right there."

The night watchman nodded, stood up, and walked away.

Floyd stood up and pulled on the slacks he had laid out neatly on the polished floor the night before. He glanced along the shadowy row of sleeping players. Nobody was stirring. Nobody had heard.

Floyd and the Falcons had watched the Fort Garrison Grizzlies—a tall, tall outfit—roll over the Smithville Tigers with ease and win their way into the championship game against the Falcons. Through the game, Jimmy seemed apart from the others. Or the others seemed apart from Jimmy. Which was it? Floyd did not know. After the game, when the last of the fans had cleared out, Floyd and the players gathered the tumbling mats and blankets from the supply room and laid out their beds along the free-throw line. Nobody said much about the Grizzlies, but Floyd knew that his players' thoughts were filled with very tall opponents wearing royal blue uniforms with white trim. The Grizzlies were the tallest team the Falcons had seen all season. The night passed without incident, and Floyd was willing to settle for that.

Buckling his belt as he walked, Floyd padded across the court in stocking feet toward the ramp leading to the office. It was two o'clock in the afternoon in Saudi Arabia. Joe Gunn had returned from his overnight trip to the construction site, had received Floyd's message, and was returning the call. Floyd tried to clear his mind of the fogginess of sleep as he walked along the ramp.

He entered the small office and closed the door behind him. He sat down at the desk, and for a moment stared at the telephone receiver, off the hook, awaiting him. Then he picked it up.

"Mr. Gunn?"

"This is Joe Gunn." The connection was good. The voice from Saudi Arabia, vaguely familiar to Floyd from their one conversation, came through clearly. "Did I wake you? I know it's early there."

"Yes, but that's all right. I'm glad you've called."

"What's wrong?"

The abrupt question caught Floyd by surprise. But of course Joe Gunn thought something was wrong. Why else would Floyd place a telephone call halfway around the world to a man he had met only once? And besides, Jimmy's mother had asked the same question. She had not pressed Floyd, but she surely had her suspicions, and she must have expressed them to her husband.

Before Floyd could answer, Joe Gunn said, "I've spoken to my wife. She said you were going to be calling me, something about placing a call to Jimmy to boost morale." He paused a second, then added, "She seemed to think there might be more to it than that."

"Yes," Floyd said, marshaling his thoughts.

"She also told me that you won your first two games, and now you're going after the championship. That's great. Congratulations."

Floyd sighed. "Thank you," he said.

"But there's a problem," Joe Gunn stated flatly.

"Yes, there is a problem," Floyd said slowly. "And I'm calling to ask a favor of you . . . a favor for all of us, but most of all, I think, a favor for Jimmy."

Floyd sketched the history of the problems with Jimmy, dating his account from the day that Joe Gunn had come to him with the word of Jimmy's unhappiness. Floyd tried to choose his words carefully, but there was no way to avoid describing the sneers, the arrogant shrugs, the cutting remarks. They were the ingredients of the worsening situation throughout the season. Floyd paused several times in the telling. He hoped for a word of encouragement, a phrase of understanding, from the man at the other end of the telephone line. He got only silence during his pauses. Unable to see Joe Gunn's face, and receiving no comments, Floyd had no way of knowing how he was taking this tale of troubles. Floyd worried that he had made a terrible mistake. Joe Gunn might not appreciate hearing bad news about Jimmy. He might blame Floyd and strike back in defense of his son. He might make matters worse. But Floyd was nearing the end of his narrative. He paused again after describing the blowup in the dressing room after the Warren Tech game.

This time Jimmy's father spoke. "I see," he said.

"And then last night, after we won, Jimmy tried to quit the team."

"Quit?" There was a tone of alarm in Joe Gunn's voice.

"He hurried out of the shower, dressed before the

126

others, and told me he was going home, quitting, walking out."

"Did he do it?"

"I talked him out of it."

The line was silent a moment. Joe Gunn was waiting.

"But the problem of Jimmy and the others is still there," Floyd said.

"And you're playing for the championship tonight."

"Yes."

"What is it that you want me to do?"

Floyd swallowed hard. This was the difficult part. He had to say words he did not like saying and ask for a favor that he did not like having to request. He had no way of knowing whether Joe Gunn would agree with his proposal. And even if he did agree, Floyd had no way of knowing whether Joe Gunn could carry it off. Could Joe Gunn sway his son? Floyd didn't know, but he plunged ahead. There was nothing else to do.

"I want you to call Jimmy and make him proud that he is a member of the Cedar Grove Falcons basketball team. I want you to make him proud that he is from a very small school that has beaten two of the best big-school teams in the state, and can beat another one and win the championship. I want you to make him proud, not ashamed, that his uniform is faded and that we don't have warm-up suits. We've slept on tumbling mats on the basketball court because we didn't have room reservations and—"

"Really?"

Floyd thought he detected a smile in Joe Gunn's voice. "Yes," he said, "but that's another story."

"That's great! You actually slept on the basketball court where you had knocked off those big-town teams?"

"Yes."

"I really think that's great."

"That's what I want you to tell Jimmy, that it was great. I want you to make him proud, not ashamed, that we slept on the basketball court."

"Uh-huh, yes."

Floyd paused a moment. He leaned forward over the desk, holding the telephone to his ear with his left hand. The fingers of his right hand were drumming the desktop. He thought he was winning Joe Gunn's agreement.

"The first move to mend this problem has got to come from Jimmy," Floyd said. "Jimmy has knocked everything about us all season—our uniforms, our gym, even the personal appearance of some of his teammates. He's ashamed to be a part of us. He's embarrassed by being a part of our team. The other players know it and they resent it." Floyd took a breath. "Jimmy can turn it around, I think. I hope that the other players will accept an overture from him, a change in his way of thinking. But he's got to prove it to them, he's got to want to prove it to them. And he can't do it until he is proud, really proud, of what we've all done together." Floyd stopped talking.

The line was silent so long that Floyd feared he had lost the connection. "Hello," he said finally.

"I'm here," Joe Gunn said. "You must be one heck of a guy."

Floyd blinked at the unexpected flattery. "No," he said. "If I were a heck of a guy I would not have to be calling for your help. But I've got a heck of a basket-ball team, and Jimmy is an important part of it. It would be tragic if everything fell apart . . . more tragic for Jimmy than anyone else."

"I understand," Jimmy's father said. "Yes, I see. And I understand what you want. And, sure, I'll give it a try. Of course, I will. No guarantees, you under-stand, but I'll give it a try."

Floyd was unconsciously nodding his head as Joe Gunn spoke. This was what he wanted, and what he—and Jimmy and all the other Falcons—needed. Floyd could ask no more.

"I know it will work," Floyd said. "It's obvious that Jimmy has a great deal of respect for you . . . and he cares a great deal what you think. He will listen to you."

"I think so . . . I hope so," Joe Gunn said softly. Then he added, "We'll give it a try."

"Good, great," Floyd said. "I'd like you to call him today a little after six-thirty our time, if you could. I know that's awfully late for you there . . . the middle of the night, I guess, but . . ."

"No problem," Joe Gunn said.

129

"Well, that's the time we'll be gathering in the dressing room to get ready for the game, with all of us in there together, and—"

"Believe me, it's no problem. I'm used to making allowances for the time difference. No problem at all."

"Fine," Floyd said. "And thanks."

They hung up.

Floyd sat for a moment with his hand still on the telephone. He was beginning to believe that Joe Gunn could pull it off. But that led to another question: Could Jimmy pull it off with his teammates?

Floyd glanced at his watch. Almost six-thirty. Twelve hours to go.

Fifteen

When Floyd and the players returned from breakfast,
Gene's father was waiting for them at courtside.

"Have you seen the papers?" he asked.

Floyd shook his head.

"The papers in Little Rock are calling Eddie the
best college prospect in the whole tournament," Wilson Montgomery announced with a smile on his face.

"Me?" Eddie said. He seemed genuinely surprised.

"Really?" Gene said. "Wow!"

Floyd smiled. "That's good," he said. But he was
not sure he believed his own words. He was not at all
certain that he liked the idea of newspaper stories
praising Eddie's prospects as a college player. Not
right now, anyway. Floyd could still hear the words
going around town: "Floyd's just taking the Falcons
to the Class A tournament to showcase his brother for
a college scholarship and maybe get himself a job at a
bigger school." Floyd did not know how many of the
people of Cedar Grove believed the charge. He did

not know how many of his players believed the charge. But he was sure that his players, barely hours before playing for the championship, did not need reminders of the gossip to distract them now.

"And they say that Jimmy is a cinch to make the all-tournament team, too," Gene's father added.

Floyd was grateful for the postscript. "Fine," he said. "That's fine." He glanced at Jimmy, but his face showed nothing. Perhaps the big-city boy expected no less than all-tournament honors. After all, he was playing with a team of hicks lucky enough to have made their way into the championship game. Floyd, watching Jimmy's impassive face, hoped that Joe Gunn realized how much was riding on one telephone conversation scheduled for later in the day.

"Let me have the keys to your van," Wilson Montgomery said, "and we'll cruise around town and meet you back here for lunch. I know you've got a lot of work to do."

"Sure," Floyd said. "I'll walk out with you."

The players ambled across the court, heading for the ramp leading to the lobby.

"Was there another problem with Jimmy last night?" Wilson Montgomery asked in a low tone as he and Floyd dropped back from the group of players. "Last night, I mean, when I ran into you and Jimmy in the corridor and . . ."

Floyd smiled at him and said, "You're pretty perceptive. Yes, Jimmy tried to quit the team."

"Quit? Now? With the championship game tonight?"

"I think I talked him out of it. Nobody else knows about it."

"Okay," Gene's father said slowly, sounding concerned. He glanced ahead at the players, seeking out Jimmy. Floyd followed his gaze. Jimmy again seemed apart from the others walking across the lobby to the front door.

The two men walked in silence for a moment. Then Gene's father said, "Everybody in town is really talking up the idea of coming up for the game tonight."

"Really? Are they serious?"

Wilson Montgomery chuckled softly. "I think they are. I think they really are."

Floyd was surprised. He had dismissed the earlier mention of a caravan as just so much chatter. It was natural in the wake of the big victory over Warren Tech. But it wasn't going to happen. The people of Cedar Grove were small farmers and small businessmen. They had neither the time nor the money to drive three hours just to see a basketball game, and then drive three hours back home. Cedar Grove, lacking a history of championship teams, had never caught basketball fever. Wild-eyed fans who drove over endless miles of highway to cheer their team came with a championship tradition, and the Falcons had never won a championship. Aside from that, the discomforting rumbles about Floyd's motives in leading the Falcons to the Class A tournament had more than cooled the send-off for the team. No, Floyd could not believe that there was going to be a caravan of Cedar Grove townspeople arriving to watch their

133

Falcons play—even in the championship game.

"Everybody was talking about it when I stopped at Big John's for a cup of coffee on the way out of town this morning."

Floyd said nothing for a moment. Then he spoke the question in his mind. "Big John," he said, "was he there?"

Gene's father laughed. "At six o'clock in the morning? You know better than that." Then he added, "But the early birds at the window table were all talking about the folks planning to drive up for the game."

"Ummm," Floyd said. "Well, I hope so. I hope they do. It would mean a lot to the boys."

"Wait a minute," Gene's father said, stopping. Floyd stopped and stood with him. Ahead of them, the players were pushing their way through the double doors leading outside. "I don't think you understand."

"What do you mean?"

"Everybody is mighty proud of the Falcons."

"Big John, too?"

Gene's father had a knowing look, a sort of amused glint in his eye. "I think you're in for a surprise when it comes to Big John," he said.

Floyd watched the other man. He decided not to press the issue. He said only, "Okay," and they resumed walking across the lobby.

At the front door Floyd handed the van keys to Gene's father and leaned out the door behind him.

"See you later," he called to his players. "And I should know some more by then about that team from—where is it?—the team we're playing tonight."

Gene laughed and waved. Eddie smiled. Gene's father unlocked the van and the players piled in.

Floyd turned and walked toward the office. He knew the three coaches he needed to reach. They were the three coaches—the only three—whose teams had whipped the very tall Fort Garrison Grizzlies during the regular season. And he knew the first question he wanted to ask each of them: "Was your team shorter than the Grizzlies?" There had to be a way for the Falcons to overcome the Grizzlies' height advantage. If just one of the coaches answered yes, Floyd would figure he had struck gold.

Floyd struck gold on the second call.

"Yes, we were shorter," said the coach of the Franklin Ridge Panthers.

"How did you beat them?"

"In a word, luck." The coach chuckled. "They're not only big, they're good."

"I'm afraid I'm going to need more than luck," Floyd said. "I'm just about fresh out of luck."

In fact, there was more than luck involved in the Franklin Ridge victory over the Fort Garrison Grizzlies. For almost thirty minutes Floyd listened to the Franklin Ridge coach and listed the ingredients of the Panthers' victory. Throughout the monologue, two words kept recurring, *shoot* and *turnovers*. The Pan-

135

thers had won by outracing the taller and slower Grizzlies, and by shooting and hitting from the outside, over their high, high reach.

"But," the Franklin Ridge coach cautioned, "your boys are only going to get one shot at a time. Their big center—and those big fowards, too—are going to sweep the boards clean every time. They're going to get the rebounds. Your boys have got to hit when they shoot. And on defense, well, they've got to force turnovers—steals, interceptions, fumbles—before the Grizzlies have a chance to get set under the basket."

Floyd liked the suggestion of a running game. His Falcons knew how to run. They had demonstrated that fact to the Melville Heights Bulldogs. They could move the ball and do it quickly. As for scoring on the first shot, Floyd kept seeing Jimmy Gunn's face. Jimmy, hot from the corner, was capable of hitting on seven or eight out of ten shots. The defense advice— force turnovers—was good advice for any game. The quick hands and feet of the twins had forced midcourt turnovers all season long. They knew how to do it.

Floyd scribbled notes while the coach talked—individual strengths and weaknesses of the Grizzlies— and came to the end of the conversation with mixed feelings. The Grizzlies doubtless were going to be the toughest team the Falcons had faced, and the battle was going to be a hard one. But the Grizzlies' vulnerabilities and weaknesses fitted neatly against the Falcons' strengths. A tough game, yes, but there was reason for optimism.

"They can be whipped," the Franklin Ridge coach said in closing. "But it won't be easy."

Floyd thanked him and hung up the telephone.

A half-hour later Floyd hung up the telephone again, this time after talking to the third and last coach on his list. He leaned back in the chair and stared at the far wall. His mind was full of tall Fort Garrison players with their hands all over the backboard, the twins grabbing interceptions, Jimmy firing in jump shots from the corner, the noise of the crowd, the glittering brightness of the court at game time.

The door opened and a stranger's face appeared. "Oh, there you are," he said. "They told me I'd probably find you in one of the offices."

"Yes?"

"Do you have a minute?" The man walked into the office as he spoke. "I know you're awfully busy, a lot to do, but just a minute?"

Floyd looked at the man. He was slightly older than Floyd, probably in his middle or late twenties. He stood around six feet four and had an athletic build. He was not too far removed from his playing days. The man smiled at Floyd in a friendly way.

"What can I do for you?" Floyd asked.

"I'm Jeffrey Bradley," he said, as he extended his right hand. "We haven't met before. I'm on the staff at Anderson University."

"Oh," Floyd said slowly. He found himself getting to his feet and taking Jeffrey Bradley's hand. They shook. Floyd knew about Anderson University. The

137

Oklahoma school was a national powerhouse in college basketball every year. But what was this man doing here? Why did he want to see Floyd? And why now? Floyd repeated his question, "What can I do for you?"

The door behind Bradley remained open. Floyd hoped that meant that he did indeed want only a minute of his time, and would be leaving. Floyd had work to do.

As if the man were reading Floyd's mind, he said, "Only a minute, I promise." He continued to smile. "We always scout the tournament," he continued. "We scout a lot of them." He shrugged his shoulders easily. "Recruiting, you know."

Floyd nodded. He thought he saw what was coming.

"And, well, I know that you probably won't be around for long after the game tonight, and you'll have your hands full anyway, and I knew that if I was going to meet you at all, well, it had to be now. And I did want to meet you."

"Yes," Floyd said. Then, after an awkward pause, he gestured at a chair alongside the desk. "Have a seat."

Bradley sat down, and Floyd sat in the chair behind the desk.

"I won't keep you a minute," he promised again. "It's about your brother, Eddie. He's quite good. He's got excellent prospects. Has he selected a school yet?"

Floyd picked up a pencil and tapped the eraser

lightly on the desktop. "No," he said, staring at the pencil. "No, he hasn't. We've hardly talked about it." He paused. "I know it's time we started thinking about it," he added.

"I've never heard of Cedar Grove," Bradley said. His friendly smile remained in place.

"Uh-huh," Floyd said, returning the smile. "Not many people have, I guess."

"Until now."

"What?"

"You're on the map now," the man said.

"I never thought of it that way."

"I'm not the first to ask about Eddie, am I?"

"Yes, as a matter of fact, you are."

"There'll be others. Eddie's been handling himself like a master all through this tournament—and facing the best teams in the state. He's a real prospect." Bradley paused. "There'll be others asking. You can bet on it."

"Eddie will be interested in listening. He's going to college, and he wants to play ball."

"I hope he will consider Anderson. We're out of state, that's true. But we're right next door, not far from home. And we've got a great program."

"I know you do."

Bradley leaned toward Floyd. Before he spoke, Floyd knew his voice was going to drop a notch or two in volume. And Floyd knew, for some reason he could not identify, that he was not going to like what he was about to hear.

"One other thing, coach, and then I'll be on my

way and let you get your work done." He paused. "You've got a lot of talent we might be interested in. That Montgomery boy, good floor player, good play-maker. And the Gunn boy, one of the smoothest shooters I've seen. They're juniors, aren't they? The twins, too, are pretty polished for sophomores."

Floyd nodded without speaking.

"They might like to follow their coach after high school," the man said.

Floyd waited.

"We've got a growing program at Anderson," Bradley continued, "and we're always on the lookout for bright young coaches for assistant jobs." He paused. "I don't know if you are planning to spend your entire career coaching at Cedar Grove, but if Eddie chose Anderson and you were interested in moving up, we might . . ."

The man's voice trailed off in Floyd's mind. A sense of shock closed off his hearing. He knew that big-time college basketball recruiting got rough, that the bids ran high for prize talent. He knew that Eddie was a prize. And behind Eddie, Gene and Jimmy, and maybe the twins, too. But still the suggestion that he would deliver Eddie and maybe the promise of the others in return for a job came as a shock to him.

But the shock was nothing compared to the jolt Floyd got when he saw, just beyond Jeffrey Bradley's shoulder, Gene Montgomery standing in the door staring, his mouth open.

Sixteen

Gene found his voice quickly. "Dad wanted me to tell you that we're back and we're going over to lunch, if you want to come with us."

The last phrase—"if you want to come with us"—hit Floyd like a dash of cold water in the face. Gene had heard Jeffrey Bradley's proposal. He had seen Floyd listening. Did he think Floyd was trying to wangle a deal to leave Cedar Grove with Eddie and maybe the others, too, as bait? Floyd was afraid he knew the answer.

"Maybe," Floyd told Gene, trying hard to seem casual. "But I've got a lot of paper work to do on the game plan. You all go on without me. I'll join you if I can."

Gene glanced at Jeffrey Bradley, who was now standing. Then he looked back at Floyd. He nodded once and left.

Floyd stood up, hoping the move would hurry Jeffrey Bradley out of the office. "I'm sure Eddie will keep Anderson in mind," he said.

The man looked back at the empty doorway. "I hope—"

"No problem," Floyd said. "Don't worry about it."

Bradley's smile returned. "Good, okay." He extended his hand and Floyd took it. "Good luck tonight. Fort Garrison is tough, but I'm betting you can pull it off."

"Thanks."

The man left. Floyd remained standing behind the desk. His first impulse was to chase after Gene. But no, he would catch up with him at the van where the others were waiting. What then? Pull Gene aside for an explanation while the others watched and wondered from a distance? No, no. Then what? Perhaps explain what had happened to everyone, Gene and all of them together. But again, no. Somehow the picture of himself running up to them, puffing, to say—what? That a college coach had expressed interest in Eddie? What was wrong with that? Or even that a college coach had expressed interest in Floyd? What was wrong with that? Plenty when considered in the context of what Gene had heard.

Floyd finally sat down. His shoulders slumped. He felt like a juggler who had kept three balls in the air, and then four balls, and now had to try to keep five balls in the air—knowing all the while that he could not do it. The fifth ball was going to make him drop them all.

Floyd turned the chair sideways and leaned back, stretching his legs out in front of him, and stared through the open door. He could see Gene's face there in the door openmouthed, staring.

Then Floyd turned back to the desk. He stood and gathered the pages of notes together. He folded them once, then twice, and jammed them in his hip pocket. He walked out the door. He had work to do.

As for what Gene had overheard, he knew now what had to be done—but later, later.

Don Benson intercepted Floyd as he walked along the edge of the basketball court. "Well, you've got your fans coming in for the game tonight, I see," Benson said with a wide grin.

"What's that?" Floyd asked, stopping and turning to face him.

"We got a call from . . . let's see, I've got the name here somewhere . . . asking if tickets were still available." Benson fumbled through a pocket notebook. "John Raymond," he said. "That's it, John Raymond. You know him, I guess."

"Really?" Floyd said. The tone of his voice revealed his surprise. Then he added, "Sure, that's Big John."

"Big John, huh?" Benson said. "Well, he sure thinks big."

"What do you mean?"

"He asked if we could hold four hundred tickets for him."

143

"Four hundred!"

"Yep, four hundred. I told him that sure, we could hold them back from the ticket booth for him until six-thirty. We'll try to do anything for a team in the championship game. But at six-thirty, if he hasn't claimed them, I'll have to release them."

Floyd ran a hand through his hair. "Four hundred," he repeated. He remembered Gene's father saying there was talk about people coming to the game and remarking that Big John might surprise him. But four hundred people was unbelievable. "That's just about everybody in the whole town of Cedar Grove," Floyd mumbled.

"Well," Benson said, "sounds like they're coming. But we can't hold the tickets past six-thirty. That's when the crowd begins to really hit the ticket windows. He said—what's his name? Big John?—he said they'd be here by then."

"Jeez," Floyd said in amazement. Then a thought popped into his head. "Look, Mr. Benson," he said. "If they're not here by six-thirty—you know, something might delay them a few minutes or so—I'll take responsibility for the tickets. Let me have them and I'll hold them for the folks from Cedar Grove. Okay?"

Benson frowned briefly. Then he said, "I guess so. Yeah, that'll be okay. Sure."

"Thanks," Floyd said. "Thanks for your help."

"Think nothing of it. Oh, by the way"—he paused and grinned again—"are you going to be needing the floor again tonight, or will you be going home after the game?"

144

Floyd had not thought about it, but he took only a moment to answer. "We'll be going home after the game," he said.

Floyd was still sitting in the stands halfway up the huge bowl when the players walked in. He had skipped lunch, leaving the team in the care of Gene's father. The lunch hour had long since passed, but Floyd had not worried about the players. Wilson Montgomery was sure to keep them occupied during the afternoon. Now the afternoon was running out and the hour was late. Floyd had sheets of papers with his notes on them spread out on the grandstand seats around him. Somehow the thinking came easier and better for him in the arena. The desk in the office offered more working space, but here Floyd could look up from his notes and see why they were important—the glistening hardwood floor, the hoops with the nets hanging limply, the glass backboards. Floyd was like a general who planned a battle better in the field than in an office behind the lines. As the general in his imagination could sniff the smoke and hear the clamor of battle, sitting in the arena Floyd could hear the *thump-thump-thump* of a dribbler, hear the sound—*punk!*—of ball hitting backboard, and hear the deafening roar of the crowd.

Floyd did not notice the players and Gene's father emerging from the ramp until Eddie shouted, "Hey!"

Floyd looked up and waved. "Be right there," he called out. He gathered up his papers and moved down the row of seats to the court.

145

He looked at his players as he walked along the sideline of the court toward them. Jimmy's difference from the other players was always striking—his haircut, his clothes, even the way he stood—and again, he seemed to be standing apart from the rest of them. The others, all of them boys Floyd had known since they were toddlers and he was in grade school, looked like every Cedar Grove boy he had ever known—jeans, work shoes, mackinaw jackets, close-cropped hair. And here they were in the giant Talbott State arena with a chance to become champions. Unconsciously, Floyd smiled at them as he approached.

"Let's go into the dressing room where we can close the door," he said. "We've got some things to talk about."

The players turned and headed for the ramp. Surely Gene had told them what he had seen and heard, but no one said anything. And no one—not Eddie, not the twins, not even Gene—revealed anything in their expressions.

Gene's father and Floyd, as if responding to a silent signal, hung back and fell into stride together far behind the players.

Floyd glanced expectantly at the other man. He knew what was coming.

"Gene heard somebody—he didn't know who or from where—talk to you about taking another job," Gene's father said.

"I know," Floyd said. "What did the players say? Were they upset?"

Gene's father walked a couple of paces in silence

146

before answering. "No," he said finally, "not upset. But they were concerned . . . maybe distracted is a better word. You know, this comes after all that talk around town that you were just interested in trying to get Eddie a scholarship and maybe a job for yourself. And, well . . ."

"And that I'd risk letting them be embarrassed to give it a try."

"Yes."

"But they've won two games. They beat probably the best team in the state on the first night. Now they're playing for the championship. That's a long way from getting themselves embarrassed."

"That's what I told them."

"Did they accept that?"

Wilson Montgomery shrugged his shoulders. "Who knows?" They stopped short of the dressing-room door. The players had gone in. "You know," he continued, "Eddie is the only senior on the starting team. All the others will be returning next year. It's a little unsettling to a player to hear that his coach may not be returning with him next year."

"Yes," Floyd said. "I understand."

"It's just that, well, they don't need these kinds of distractions when they're going into the championship game."

"You're right about that," Floyd said. "Let's go in."

Floyd, ushering Gene's father in ahead of him, closed the dressing-room door and took up a stance beside it. The players were scattered about on benches and on the training table. Floyd thrust his hands in his pockets and tried to convey a casual image. He looked around at his players, and the sight reassured him. They looked serious but not worried. Despite all the problems, the honorary assistant coach had succeeded in bringing the players through an active but relaxing day leading up to the game.

"First," Floyd said, "let's talk about something that has nothing at all to do with tonight's game." A questioning expression appeared on the faces in front of him. Floyd paused a moment and then asked, "Any of you been approached by a college coach since we've been here?"

The questioning expressions changed to looks of surprise.

"You, Eddie?" Floyd looked at his brother. "You're a senior. Has any college coach spoken to you?"

"No."

"Any of the rest of you?"

Around the semicircle the players shook their heads.

"Good," Floyd said. Out of the corner of his eye he saw Gene's father watching him with a puzzled expression. "Well, I was approached today." He smiled and added, "Yes, me." The faces in front of him showed interest. "It came as a surprise to me, and the reason I'm asking if you've had any contacts is because the NCAA has clear and specific rules on the matter, and you should be aware of them. There is a limit to the contact that college coaches can have with high-school prospects, and I don't want any of you to jeopardize your futures by not knowing this.

You're good enough to be playing for the state championship tonight, and so you're certainly good enough to attract the attention of college scouts. Just let me know if anyone approaches you. Okay?"

The players nodded. Floyd watched Gene. The boy's steady gaze seemed to tell Floyd that he was halfway to putting the episode of the Anderson coach out of everyone's mind.

"There's nothing wrong with a college coach asking if you've decided where you're going to school, or even urging you to consider his school. That's all fair and aboveboard." Floyd paused a moment. "But you should understand that some of them can suggest some pretty funny arrangements. They can hint at some pretty wild things, just as the one who approached me today did, and I need to know for your own good when and if this happens to you. Okay?"

Floyd looked around. He could sense that he had succeeded. He was sure of it. The players were nodding their agreement. And Gene's father, leaning against a locker at the far side of the dressing room, was smiling at him.

"Now," Floyd said, "about this team we're going to play tonight."

Seventeen

The dressing room was quiet. The players were peeling off their street clothes and getting into their game uniforms—the faded red shirts, the faded black trunks. The muffled roar of the crowd sifted through the ceiling of the room. Seated on the training table, Floyd was reminded again of the sound of distant thunder across the hills around Cedar Grove. He glanced at his wristwatch. The time was almost a quarter to seven. Time was running out for the telephone call from Saudi Arabia. Floyd ran a hand through his hair.

Suddenly the dressing-room door flew open and the head of a stranger appeared. "Jimmy Gunn?" a man said, looking around. He found Jimmy, familiar from the games of the previous two nights. "You've got a phone call in the office—from Saudi Arabia!"

The players, all now nearly dressed, looked around in surprise.

"Arabia!" Gene Montgomery said.

"My father?" Jimmy asked, puzzled.

"C'mon," the man said. "They're on the line."

Jimmy, in his uniform but still barefoot, followed the man into the corridor.

"Wow!" Gene said. "Nobody ever called me from Arabia."

"I wouldn't even call you from Little Rock," Eddie said with a grin.

Floyd smiled absently at Eddie's wisecrack. But his thoughts were down the corridor in the small office, where a telephone line was open to Saudi Arabia. Floyd's telephone scouting had been done. His battle plan had been drawn. The strategy had been explained to the players. And now, at this moment, the final tactic for victory—perhaps the most vital one of all—was being fitted into place. This tactic, unlike the others Floyd had scribbled in pencil on lined yellow pages, had the sole purpose of making the Falcons a team again. Floyd felt a sense of helplessness. This play was unfolding out of his earshot, beyond his control.

The players were dressed and ready to take the court for their warm-up drills when Jimmy returned. He stepped inside and closed the dressing-room door behind him. He stood without moving and looked around the room for a moment. He seemed on the brink of speaking, but said nothing.

"C'mon, get your shoes on," Floyd said. He tried to sound casual. "It's getting late."

Jimmy nodded. "Yeah, sure," he said. He walked to the bench and sat down, and began pulling on a sock.

Floyd watched him. He had no way of knowing what either Joe Gunn or his son had said to each other. He could not tell what effect the conversation had had on Jimmy, if any. Jimmy's face gave no clue. He was busily pulling on socks and shoes.

"Well, what did he say?" Gene finally piped up. "He's been reading about us in all the Arabian papers, and he . . ."

Floyd could have hugged Gene. The icebreaker was perfect. If Jimmy's father had succeeded, Gene's joking way of asking the question opened the door for Jimmy.

Jimmy looked up at Gene. For a moment he seemed unsure of what to say. Then he returned Gene's grin. "Well, I thought he was going to laugh his head off about our sleeping on the basketball court the last two nights. My mother had told him about it."

Floyd almost flinched. The mention of the team sleeping on the floor brought back unpleasant memories—the blowup the first night, the cold stares the second night. But a quick glance at Jimmy eased Floyd's mind. Jimmy was still grinning, and his eyes were sparkling.

The dressing-room door opened a crack and somebody called out, "Time, coach."

"Okay," Floyd called back. "Right there."

Jimmy leaned forward in his seat on the bench, looking around at the players. He was not smiling now, but his face seemed wiped clean of the uncertainty of a moment ago. "My father asked me to tell you, all of you, that he knows how proud we all are, all of us, to be a team from a little school that nobody ever heard of, having the . . ." Jimmy paused, ". . . having the confidence and the courage to go up against the big schools, and . . ." he paused again, "and the skills and determination to beat the big schools."

Floyd sat motionless on the training table. It seemed that Joe Gunn had succeeded. What remained was to find out whether Jimmy was able to succeed. Joe Gunn had changed Jimmy's mind. Could Jimmy change the minds of his teammates? Could he do it with one statement?

Floyd scanned the faces of his players. Eddie, seated on a bench, was staring at Jimmy with a slight frown. His expression seemed to say that he knew he was watching a new Jimmy Gunn. Roy was nodding his head slightly. Ray was listening with the look of one having trouble believing his ears. Gene was the easiest for Floyd to read. With the beginning of a smile on his face, Gene did not seem at all surprised. He looked as if he had always known Jimmy would come around.

"Well, that's what he said," Jimmy finished. Then, speaking barely above a whisper, he said, "And he's right." He looked up. "You know, we're really something."

Floyd exhaled. He felt he had been holding his breath for an hour. He sent out a silent salute to the

153

man named Joe Gunn in Saudi Arabia, and he sent out another to the basketball player named Jimmy Gunn.

Gene, grinning, said, "Yeah, man!"

Jimmy pulled out the front of his shirt and looked down at it, saying nothing.

Maybe, Floyd thought, the faded colors didn't matter any longer.

"Let's go," Floyd said, hopping down from the training table.

Gene's father met them just outside the dressing-room door. "The whole town is here," he announced. The excitement showed on his face. "The whole town," he repeated.

The players gathered around Gene's father and Floyd.

"Don Benson told me he had received calls about tickets," Floyd said.

"Well, I guess Benson got the tickets for them, and everybody—and I do mean everybody, the whole town—is here."

Floyd blinked. "The *whole* town?"

"Everybody, everybody," Gene's father said. "They even had to hire an off-duty deputy from over at Mason to watch things—you know, vandalism and fires and things like that—so the volunteer firemen on call and the marshal could come, too." The words tumbled out in rapid-fire order. "They all came in a caravan, just poured through the front door all together. I ran into them in the lobby. Everybody's here, everybody."

The players looked at Floyd.

"That's great," Floyd said softly. "Really great."

When the Falcons walked out the end of the ramp and stepped to the edge of the court, a giant roar filled the arena. Everyone—all sixteen thousand fans, it seemed—were on their feet cheering.

"*Fal-cons! Fal-cons!*" came the roar from all sides.

The fans were sticking with the favorite they had adopted—the Falcons, the small squad with the faded uniforms and the young coach with the sprig of hair standing up in the back.

The first thing Floyd saw was a red light atop a television camera on a motorized tricycle backing up slowly in front of him. Floyd stared into the camera for a moment and then, with his players, walked around the camera to the bench.

Looking up, he then saw the Cedar Grove fans, seated together, midway up the stands opposite the bench. They were easy to spot. There was a lot of red, almost a solid mass of red covering the bloc of seats. Truly, the whole town of Cedar Grove must be here. Somebody had brought one of the banners from school—CLASS A—ALL THE WAY—and it was stretched out along a row. Floyd wanted to wave. They were the friends he had known all his life. But he only nodded in acknowledgment and turned to his players.

155

"There are the folks from your town," he said. "Look at them . . . and then forget them. We've got a game to play."

Then he sent his players onto the court for their warm-up drills.

At the other end of the court the Fort Garrison Grizzlies already were into their drills, dribbling, passing, shooting. Floyd stood for a moment watching them. He had seen them play last night, had talked on the telephone all morning with people who knew them, and had spent the afternoon shuffling facts about them. Now in the bright glare of the final minutes before the opening tip-off, he had nothing more to learn about the Grizzlies. He glanced back at his own players, taking their shots and walked to the scorer's table with his lineup.

Don Benson was there with the Fort Garrison coach.

"Coach Bentley, Coach Carrington."

Floyd barely heard the words above the roar of the crowd, as he shook hands with Carrington. The man looked hardly older than Floyd, but Floyd knew that Marsh Carrington was in his fourth year as the Grizzlies' coach and was no stranger to the state tournament. The Grizzlies had lost in the semifinals the year before.

"Good luck, Floyd," Carrington said. He spoke in a friendly way, sounding as if he and Floyd had been friends for years.

"Luck to you, too, Marsh," Floyd said.

"Now," Benson said, "when you come back out of the dressing room, as you know, we're going to be introducing the starting players individually as we always do in the championship game."

Floyd didn't know. But then he had a vague recollection from a championship game he had watched on television when he was a junior at Morrison State. The thought had not occurred to him then that he would be the man in front of the camera, sending his own players onto the court, two years later.

Benson explained the procedure, forwards first, then the center, then the guards, each team taking up a position at its own end of the court.

The two coaches nodded their understanding.

"Good luck to both of you," Benson said with an upbeat lilt in his voice.

Back in the dressing room for the final moment before taking the court for the opening tip-off, Floyd stood in the middle of the floor. He ran a hand nervously through his hair. The sprig of hair in the back went down under the weight of his hand and then sprang back up. The players were seated on benches around him.

"I've never been much for pep talks," he said. "You all know that."

Eight serious faces were turned up toward him.

"I guess that I'm supposed to say that this is just another game, and you should just go out there and play your normal way. But that's not true. This is not just another game. You are going out there tonight to play for the state championship. This is the biggest game you've ever played. Maybe the biggest you will ever play. You're going to remember this game, every little detail of it, for the rest of your lives."

Floyd consciously resisted the impulse to run his hand through his hair again. "You can win this game and the championship. You know it and I know it. You've already whipped what's probably the best team in the state. That was Warren Tech. You can whip this team tonight. It'll be great to win . . . and be the state champions."

Floyd stopped and took a breath. "But that's not the point of what I want to tell you. I want you to know before we go out there that no matter how it turns out—win or lose—you are champions. You really are. In my book, you are champions right now, and you do not have to win another game to prove it."

One by one, Floyd looked at the faces staring up at him: Gene, Eddie, Jimmy, the twins, William, John, Bobby.

"Most of the people in Cedar Grove are up there in the seats tonight. They are here, a long, three-hour drive from home, because they are proud of you. You have made them proud. You have made me proud. And win or lose, we will come out of this game tonight proud."

Then Floyd managed to put on a confident smile that he did not feel at all. "So now," he said, "let's go out there and win the big one."

Gene gave a short pump with his clenched fist and nodded. But he was not smiling. Not this time. Nobody was smiling.

"Let's go," Floyd repeated quietly, and he stepped across and opened the dressing-room door.

Eighteen

"For the Cedar Grove Falcons . . ."

The announcer's voice booming through the loud-speakers reverberated through the giant arena for a brief moment and then lost out to the roaring cheer of the fans.

Across the court, Floyd saw the television camera turning from the Fort Garrison Grizzlies, now standing together at one end of the court, to point toward him and his Falcons standing in front of their bench.

"At the forwards, Gene Montgomery . . ." Gene raced onto the court, fists clenched in front of him. The cheers rolled down from the grandstands. The television camera turned slowly to follow him onto the court, then turned back to the bench.

". . . and Jimmy Gunn." Jimmy ran onto the court. He and Gene slapped hands. And then, before stepping back to take his place beside Gene, he put an arm around his teammate's shoulder and gave a squeeze. Gene seemed almost to be expecting the

gesture. He looked at Jimmy and nodded. Jimmy stepped away to await the next player.

"At center . . . Eddie Bentley." Eddie jogged onto the court and slapped hands with Gene and then Jimmy—and then repeated Jimmy's gesture, giving Jimmy's shoulder a squeeze. Jimmy nodded at him.

Then—Ray Barton, Roy Barton, each with a shoulder squeeze for the player ahead of him.

Floyd, his hands stuffed in his hip pockets, stood at the sideline watching the unusual ritual unfold on the court. The roar of the crowd increased with each shoulder squeeze. The Cedar Grove Falcons were telling each other something—and the fans sensed it. As for Floyd, the plague of troubles seemed at this moment to be far, far back in the past.

"And the coach of the Cedar Grove Falcons . . . Floyd Bentley."

Floyd took a couple of steps onto the court, waved, and stepped back to wait for his starters to return.

The referee was walking toward the center of the court, the ball held easily between hand and hip.

Floyd leaned forward and extended his hands to his players. They reached out and clasped.

The noise in the arena was deafening. Floyd, fairly shouting to be heard above the din, said, "Okay, champs, this is it." They pumped hands and broke the group. The five starters turned and headed onto the court. Floyd and his three substitutes backed up and sat down on the bench.

Again, the contrast on the court between the teams' uniforms was startling—the Fort Garrison

Grizzlies in brilliant royal blue with white trim, the Falcons in the dull pink of their faded red shirts and the flat gray of the faded black shorts.

The Fort Garrison center, lining up against Eddie, appeared to Floyd to be taller than the six feet seven listing in the lineup. He seemed to tower over Eddie.

The taller of the two Fort Garrison forwards, listed at six feet six, was lining up against Jimmy. He, too, seemed taller than his listed height. Jimmy, standing an even six feet tall, was dwarfed by the Fort Garrison forward.

Suddenly the whole Fort Garrison team looked as tall as pine trees. Floyd glanced at the twins. At five feet eight, they were used to everyone—even their own teammates—towering over them. But now they looked like midgets. And Gene, at five feet eleven, was six inches shorter than the Fort Garrison forward lining up against him.

Floyd wiped a hand across his forehead, trying to erase thoughts of the Grizzlies' awesome height. He leaned forward, elbows on knees, hands clasped together, and awaited the opening tip. He hoped for the last time that he had thought of everything.

The referee spun the ball into the air. Eddie and the Fort Garrison center went up.

The Fort Garrison center was above Eddie at least an inch, maybe two, and won the tip. He flicked the ball to his right, into the hands of the shorter of the Fort Garrison forwards. Floyd thought of them that way—the taller and the shorter of the forwards— even though the shorter one stood a rangy six feet five. The forward took in the ball and pivoted without dribbling.

The twins and Gene swarmed around him.

The forward, startled by the unexpected defensive press, blinked and pivoted again, searching for a way out of the trap.

Eddie and Jimmy dropped back.

Floyd remained leaning forward, clenching and unclenching his hands. A pressing defense—a full-court press, all the way from the opening tip-off to the final buzzer—was a great equalizer. The Falcons, shorter but quicker, hoped to minimize the Grizzlies' height advantage by delaying them in getting set up on offense and by forcing errors, fumbles, interceptions, bobbled dribbles. Of course, a team took risks with a full-court press. The defense, instead of backing up to protect the basket, was chasing around the full length of the court, pursuing the ball. And, by being spread out, they left gaps. A shooter in the corner was going to find himself open. But Floyd had noted that the Grizzlies for all their strengths had no deadeye shooter capable of pumping in the ball consistently from the corner. The spread-out defense also left the lane under the basket open. The Grizzlies were sure to collect some points on back-door shots—a player under the basket, behind the scampering defenders, and all alone. But Floyd was betting that his Falcons could force enough turnovers—and turn them into field goals—to outweigh the points the Grizzlies could collect from the corner or through the back door.

One of the Grizzlies' guards, spotting his teammate's dilemma in the face of the Falcons' waggling hands, raced toward him. The forward lofted a pass over the Falcons and into the hands of the guard.

Floyd unconsciously slapped his right fist into his left palm. So much for the first effort with the press.

Gene and the twins turned and ran to their defensive positions while the guard dribbled to the sideline. He dribbled in place a moment, then shot a pass to the taller of the forwards down the sideline.

Under the basket, the tall center and Eddie jockeyed for position. While the Fort Garrison center was taller, Eddie was the more muscular, clearly the stronger of the two. And based on what Floyd had seen of the Fort Garrison center the night before, Eddie was the more skilled of the two. Over the long haul of the game, strength and skill should overcome an inch or two of height advantage. Floyd hoped so.

The forward dribbled toward the corner, then stopped. He faked a pass, and Gene followed the fake. For a flicker of a second, Gene was out of position. In that brief moment the forward turned and sent a high pass toward the basket. The center went up, arms stretching high. Eddie went up with him. The Fort Garrison center's hands were higher than Eddie's. His fingertips barely caressed the ball, but it was enough. The ball bounced off the backboard and dropped through the basket.

Eddie had lost the first battle of the boards. He had lost to the combination of superior height, a perfect pass—right on target—and a perfect leap, perfectly timed.

A cheer erupted from the block of seats occupied by the Fort Garrison fans. Their Grizzlies had won the opening tip. They had escaped a surprising press. They had moved the ball in for the game's first field goal. Their team was out front.

From the Cedar Grove fans across the court, and from most of the other corners of the arena, dead silence greeted the field goal. The fans who had given up their neutrality two nights ago to cheer for Cedar Grove—"*Fal-cons! Fal-cons!*"—were still pulling for the boys wearing the faded uniforms.

On the bench Floyd mumbled to himself, "Okay, okay, it's okay." Then he stood up. He caught the eye of the twin under the basket—it was Roy—accepting the ball out of bounds from the referee to resume the play. Floyd nodded slightly. Roy nodded back.

Roy said something to Ray and threw the ball inbounds to him. Ray, without dribbling once, turned and fired an overhand pass over the center line. Running at full speed, Eddie met the ball. He did not catch it, not in the real sense, anyway. He palmed the rocketing ball, and turning, propelled it on its way downcourt. The ball headed for empty space under the basket. Jimmy, coming across, took in the pass without breaking stride. He was inside the free-throw line.

The Grizzlies, who had been backtracking in the expectation of Ray's dribbling advance, stopped dead in their tracks for a fatal second. They gawked. Then they turned and ran. But they were too late.

Jimmy, with one dribble, left the floor, sailing high. There was not a single Fort Garrison player within ten feet of him. He laid the ball on the rim of the basket. It teetered on the rim a moment, then dropped in.

Floyd, still standing, shouted, "Yeah!" Eddie ran forward and clapped a grinning Jimmy on the back. The arena rocked with cheers.

A Grizzlies' guard came rushing under the basket, carried forward by the momentum of a frantic charge that had started too late. The other Grizzlies, arms dangling at their sides, stared at the floor. They had been caught by surprise, then left behind in the race. And now the score was tied.

Floyd knew the electrifying play was worth more than the two points marked on the scoreboard. For his own players, its success softened the impact of the Grizzlies' awesome use of their height in moving from tip-off to field goal in the opening seconds. The play confirmed to the Falcons that they could run and score against the Grizzlies. And for the Grizzlies, well, the play planted some worries. Floyd certainly had no intention of sending his Falcons flying down the court with long passes in every assault on the basket. But the threat was always there, and the Grizzlies could not afford to forget it.

The guard taking the ball out of bounds under the basket glanced around with a questioning look on his face. Had the pressing defense following the opening tip-off been a preview of a full-court press? He was not sure. But if so, what was he to do? What would his teammates do?

For a moment Floyd was certain that Marsh Carrington would call a time-out. His players needed to regroup. They needed to recover from the wild chase down the court that gave the Falcons their field goal. And they needed to consider the possibility of a full-court press.

But Carrington left his players on the court.

The guard accepting the ball from the referee did not have long to wonder about the possibility of a full-court press. The Falcons let him know right away. All five Falcons patrolled the backcourt in a tightly woven zone. Nobody guarded the Grizzlies' guard with the ball. He was left alone to try to find one of his four teammates free and open. It was a tough assignment.

The shorter of the forwards raced downcourt, offering himself for a long pass over the full-court press, the best tactic for breaking up a full-court press. But Jimmy went with him, step for step. The guard decided against trying the pass.

The other forward stepped quickly into the space vacated by Jimmy and the guard zipped the ball inbounds to him. The Falcons' press shifted toward the ball and edged backward.

The Grizzlies' forward tried to dribble around Gene and Roy, but he couldn't do it. He stopped. They closed in. Using his height, he held the ball high above them. He looked around desperately, then sent a fingertip pass to a teammate. It was a floater. Ray lunged forward and swatted the ball toward the basket. Roy, peeling away from the forward at the moment of the pass, slammed on the brakes, cut to his right, and grabbed the loose ball. He was under the basket. He twirled the ball upward. It rolled off the backboard and fell through the nets.

This time Marsh Carrington called for a time-out.

"Good, good," Floyd said to the players at the bench. "But they won't be surprised next time we come flying down the court. And they won't be confused next time by the full-court press."

The players nodded.

Floyd glanced across the scorer's table at the Fort Garrison bench. Marsh Carrington was standing calmly in the center of his players, talking. Floyd did not say so, but he knew by the very fact of the time-out—with the game only a minute old—that his Falcons had knocked the Grizzlies off stride.

"You've got to beat that center," Floyd told Eddie. "You can do it. He's got an inch or two on you, but you're better than he is, and stronger. You can do it."

Eddie said nothing. He had lost his only match with the center so far. His face showed that he considered Floyd's directive to be a tall order.

"Look," Floyd said, "I know you can't tie him in knots and wrap him around your little finger. He's too big and too good for that. But you've got to neutralize him. We've got the speed for the fast break and the full-court press. We can't afford to have the center offset those advantages."

"I understand."

"Okay."

When the Grizzlies' guard stepped out of bounds to take the ball from the referee for the throw-in, his teammates began a strange maneuver. They bunched up in front of him and then spread out. Then they bunched up and spread out again. In quick tempo, they repeated the maneuver over and over again. Sometimes they would send two players out to each side. Other times they would send three one way and one the other. Or all four would spread out to the same side.

The Falcons never knew which side would be flooded with Grizzlies and which would be empty.

The guard got his pass off to the shorter of the forwards. He passed across the center stripe to the taller forward.

The Grizzlies had escaped, and the Falcons fell back into their defensive positions.

The Fort Garrison players worked the ball around the perimeter of the Falcons' defense with a series of quick passes. Ray lunged at one of them—a dangerously soft throw from one of the guards to the other—but missed. Then, without a hint of what was coming, the player with the ball dribbled twice toward the basket, halted, and shot a bounce pass down the middle to the center. The center was in front of

Eddie. He took in the bounce pass and, keeping his back to Eddie, went up. He began his turn for the shot, but he no longer had the ball. Eddie, reacting quickly, had slapped it out of his hands. The ball hit the floor. The Grizzlies' shorter forward came out of nowhere, grabbed the ball on the bounce, leaped and fired for the basket. The ball bounded back off the rim. Jimmy, moving in, leaped for the ball and got a hand on it. But that was all. He could not hold on. The deflected ball danced on the fingertips of the leaping players. The Grizzlies' taller forward got it. He came down, dribbled once, leaped, and shot. His five-foot jumper dropped through.

The scoreboard changed: Falcons 4, Grizzlies 4.

If any of the cheering fans, or even the players on the court, had chanced to look at Floyd at that instant, they would have been surprised. The Grizzlies had scored, tying the game. The scoring shot had come out of a mad scramble for the ball. Games were won and lost in such scrambles. The Falcons had lost the scramble. But Floyd was not frowning. He was nodding his approval. Eddie, with his quick reflexes, had left the taller center holding nothing but air. It was a good sign, perhaps even worth two points.

Nineteen

From there, as if a pattern had been set, the two teams battled on even terms through the end of the first quarter and into the final minute of the second quarter. The Falcons were never able to regain the lead, but the Grizzlies were never able to get themselves out in front by more than four points. After each Fort Garrison surge, the Falcons retaliated, cutting the lead to two or reducing it to zero.

It was height and tip-ins versus speed and outside shooting.

When they were able to set themselves, the Grizzlies dominated the game. On offense, they outreached, and so out-rebounded, the Falcons. Even making passes around the perimeter, they used their height to good advantage. They passed high above the outstretched hands of the leaping twins. On defense, when the Falcons allowed them to get set, the Grizzlies left them with only one surefire weapon,

171

Jimmy's jump shots from the corner. Otherwise, their height was smothering the Falcons.

However, the Falcons' full-court press was paying dividends. Four times the Falcons got the ball away from the harassed Grizzlies deep in the backcourt and scored. Ray slapped away a second pass, followed the ball under the basket, and laid it in for a field goal. Jimmy reached in and deftly lifted the ball out of the hands of a Grizzly who delayed too long deciding what to do with it. Jimmy solved the problem for him by dribbling off to the side and sinking a twelve-foot jumper. Gene picked off a dribble and passed back to Roy, who dropped in a twenty-footer. Eddie, leaping in, blocked an overhand pass before it had gone three feet, and Gene scooped up the ball and scored. And on offense, the Falcons' wild galloping—the long passes, the lengthy nonstop dribbling—left the slower Grizzlies in their wake time and again. When the Grizzlies did succeed in setting their defense, the Falcons fed the ball to Jimmy in the corner. He pumped in three straight jump shots before missing.

For Floyd at the sideline, alternating between sitting and standing, the unfolding drama on the court gave cause for both cheer and worry about the second half.

Eddie was wearing down the Grizzlies' center. His superior strength was taking its toll on the other player in the warfare under the basket and was going to offset the couple of inches of height advantage before the game was over. Floyd was sure of it. Eddie's superior skill, too, was slowly converting the center from an aggressively dominant player into a tentative one. Floyd saw the evidence of it time and again—a shying away, a hesitation in making a reach, a second's delay in his leaps. He saw it, too, in the center's eyes as the second quarter drew toward a close—an expression of timidity, a look of pleading. Floyd had seen the look many times in his playing days. A player being whipped seemed unable to avoid giving himself away with his eyes. Eddie was sure to complete the conquest in the second half if he did not get himself into foul trouble. He had two fouls charged against him. That was not bad.

But the Falcons' full-court press, while valuable, was proving expensive. Not in points. The Grizzlies did not have a deadeye corner shooter to take advantage of the Falcons' spread-out defense. Nor did they have the speed to capitalize on an unprotected basket with back-door points. But the full-court press was extracting a high price in stamina. There was no rest for the players applying it. The Falcons did not lay back and wait for the advancing opponent. They charged forward—always. In those moments when another team might wait and watch, the Falcons were pounding the floor, zipping left and right, starting, stopping, turning, leaping. It never ended. Now they were breathing heavily, the perspiration cascading off them. Floyd sensed he saw less spring, less quickness, in his players' legs. They were wearing out.

More than once Floyd glanced down the bench and

started to send William into the game. The starters needed rest. William had played well, but he was not the match of the five players on the court. And with the closeness of the game, the nip-and-tuck nature of the battle, Floyd was reluctant to give up even the slightest bit of height, speed, and skill, even for a few minutes. No, he decided, the starters were going to have to wait for the halftime for a respite.

Floyd glanced up at one of the huge scoreboards: Falcons 31, Grizzlies 34.

The Grizzlies' taller forward had just hit a short jumper from in front of the basket. Ray, out of bounds, was awaiting the ball for the inbounds throw.

The clock showed one minute and two seconds remaining before the halftime intermission.

Floyd made a rolling motion with his hand. Ray saw him and nodded. They were going for the long bomb. The Falcons were not the only ones growing weary in the torrid nonstop pace of the game. The Grizzlies were looking for a moment of rest, too. Maybe a long pass would catch them off guard. A field goal, and then another, would give the Falcons the lead at the intermission. That would help. It would provide a lift for the weary Falcons. And there was only one way to capture the lead—score.

Ray, staring blankly at Roy standing there with arms outstretched, awaiting the inbounds pass, uncorked a pass almost the full length of the court.

The Grizzlies, backpedaling into position, were ready by this time for almost anything from the wild-running Falcons. But they were not ready for Ray's fifty-foot pass. It sailed over their heads.

Jimmy ran down the sideline. On the other sideline, Gene veered toward the center, in the direction of the basket where the ball was coming down. Jimmy reached out and took in the ball. Unable to control it for a shot, he bounced the ball across to Gene. The Grizzlies were thundering in behind them, any one of them tall enough to block Gene's shot. Gene, looking up at the basket, dribbled under and laid up the ball. It dropped through.

Jimmy hugged Gene. One of the twins ran up and joined in.

The scoreboard changed: Falcons 33, Grizzlies 34.

The Falcons spread out to apply the full-court press. They each seemed to Floyd to be reaching down deep one more time to tap their dwindling supply of energy.

Somewhere they found the energy and almost won possession of the ball for their trouble. The Grizzlies' guard frittered away nine of the ten seconds allowed for the inbounds pass. He was not able to find a teammate open among the Falcons' racing feet and waggling hands. Then he got the pass off at the last second. The center took it in high above his head. Eddie challenged the center, then backpedaled into his defensive position when the center dropped off the ball to a guard.

The Grizzlies took their time moving down the court. The last minute of the first half was ticking away. Clearly, they were playing for one final shot. They wanted to go into the dressing room with the lead, three points if possible, but one point for sure. They were going to take no chances.

Their guards dribbled back near the center line, watching the clock. The twins chased them, but carefully. This was no time for a foul. The Grizzlies passed the ball back and forth. The weary Falcons seemed little inclined to make the effort, probably futile anyway, to intercept or knock a pass away.

Eleven seconds . . . ten . . . nine.

With six seconds left on the clock, the taller of the forwards leaped and shot at the edge of the keyhole. The ball hit the backboard, bounced off the rim, and fell into Eddie's hands.

Eddie turned his back on the Grizzlies' center. He dribbled a couple of steps away and glanced up at the clock.

Floyd's glance followed his brother's: two seconds remaining.

Eddie wound up and threw the ball the length of the court, aiming for the basket more than fifty feet away.

He missed everything, backboard as well as basket, and the buzzer sounded, ending the first half.

Floyd stepped out onto the court to meet his players. All around the arena the fans were on their feet. Their cheers boiled into a deafening roar. Across the court, in the large splash of red that was the townspeople of Cedar Grove, the banner CLASS A—ALL THE WAY was held high. Eddie, approaching the sideline, grinned at Floyd. "I need some work on that shot," he said. Floyd, in all the noise, read Eddie's lips more than he heard the words. He returned the grin, and nodded.

Floyd and the Falcons trooped slowly off the court toward the dressing room.

Floyd, his hands stuffed in his hip pockets, stood in front of the closed door of the dressing room. His shirttail was almost out. His necktie was loosened. His hair was mussed from too many nervous swipes of his right hand.

He waited to speak. The five starters were catching their breath and toweling off the perspiration. They were the boys who had whipped Warren Tech when the folks back home thought they were headed for humiliation. They were the boys in the faded uniforms who had sent two big-city teams packing. Now they were giving a third big-city team the game of a lifetime. They were the boys who had a greenhorn for a coach but now were playing for the championship of the state.

Floyd watched his players. There was Eddie, probably the best player in the tournament. The weight of his burden was clear on his face—he had to beat a taller opponent. His role was vital and he knew it. There were the twins, slumped back and puffing. They were leg-weary and winded. They bore the brunt of the defense. There was Jimmy. He somehow looked more like a Cedar Grove boy. The haircut was the same, but the telephone conversation with his father had changed him. Jimmy's shots from the corner were keeping the Falcons in the running for victory. Surely he knew it. And there was Gene, biting his lower lip nervously, knowing better than any of the others how very much every single play counted. Off the court, Gene Montgomery was always the first with a wisecrack. But on the court he was the steadiest of the Falcons. He, probably more than any of them, knew that in the end there was going to be one play, or maybe two or three, that would decide the victor and the championship.

Floyd looked at William Logan. "Be ready, William," he said. "You're going to see a lot of action in the second half."

William nodded. The announcement came as no surprise. He knew as well as anyone that the starters were going to need breathing spells on the bench.

Floyd turned to the others. "We're heading into probably the most important five or six minutes of the game," he said. He spoke softly, matter-of-factly. "It's been my experience that more games are won in the first five minutes of the second half than the last five minutes. One team or the other comes out of the halftime intermission, grabs the momentum, and runs off a string of points. It's the turning point of the game. From there, they hang in and win."

The players watched Floyd as he spoke. A couple of them nodded slightly. They all had heard the same words from him before, at the halftime of other games. They had seen his words proven true in one of their losses, in a half dozen of their victories.

"So work hard and concentrate," Floyd continued. "Don't let them make a run on you in the opening minutes of the second half. Let's do it to them instead." He paused. "A team can give up a run of points and still come from behind and win, but it's not the easy way."

There was nothing else to say. They knew what they had to do. Eddie, Gene, Jimmy, Roy, Ray, William, all of them.

"Let's go," Floyd said.

Twenty

Floyd stood at the sideline watching his Falcons take the last of their warm-up shots. Gene's father stood beside him.

In the crowd someone started the chant—*"Fal-cons! Fal-cons!"*—and the roar spread throughout the arena. The long banner in the crowd of people wearing red—CLASS A—ALL THE WAY—was waving in cadence with the chant.

"Can they keep up the pace?" Gene's father asked.

Floyd glanced at him. The question was a good one. The Falcons had liked the running game all season, but they had never tried to race their way through an entire game. Instead, they turned on the speed at strategic moments, then returned to a more methodical game. They were a running team, true, but only in moments of their own choosing. Against the towering Fort Garrison Grizzlies they had no choice. Speed and outside shooting were the only answers to vastly superior height.

"We'll be playing William a lot," Floyd said. "To give everybody some rest."

The referee's whistle sent the players back to their benches. Gene's father moved off into the crowd, returning to his seat. The crowd's roar continued. *"Falcons! Fal-cons!"*

From behind him, Floyd heard the shouts of the outnumbered Fort Garrison fans trying to raise a cheer for the Grizzlies. They were drowned out.

Floyd bent down and clasped the hands in the center of the circle of players. "Let's get 'em," he said. The clasped hands pumped three times and then broke apart.

The starters walked onto the court, and Floyd and his substitutes backed up and sat down on the bench.

Standing in the center circle, the referee twirled the ball into the air. Eddie and the Fort Garrison center went up. The Grizzlies' center outjumped Eddie again, tipping the ball to a guard. The guard, hardly taking the time to turn, zipped a two-handed pass down the sideline to the taller of the forwards. The forward dribbled in two steps and fired for the basket. He scored.

Floyd felt a sense of foreboding. Something different was happening. Not just the forward taking his shot before the Grizzlies got themselves set in their attack formation. True, that was out of character for them. But it was more than that. Floyd had noticed the other forward racing, shoulder to shoulder, with the center toward the basket. The Grizzlies were packing their height advantage under the boards.

That meant only one thing: They were going to fire away and count on their height to capture the rebound when the shooter missed. Eddie was in for a tough, tough second half.

The Falcons brought the ball back into play and moved down the court. But they were too slow about it and the Grizzlies ran to their defensive positions. Under the boards, Floyd's guess proved to be right. The forwards were in tight with their center, adding two more bodies, two more pairs of hands, to the battle to contain Eddie. Eddie's slow but steady gaining of dominance over the other center had not gone unnoticed. Marsh Carrington had spotted it and recognized the significance. So he was giving the center some help—a lot of it.

Gene's shot from the edge of the keyhole bounced off the rim, and the Grizzlies' strategy paid off. The shorter of the forwards, with his center blocking Eddie, got the rebound.

In the blink of an eye they pumped in another field goal, a ten-foot jump shot by a guard—38–33.

And then a tip-in, after Jimmy stepped out of bounds trying to elude a guard—40–33.

Roy's long pass inbounds was picked off by the taller of the forwards, the Grizzlies' first interception. Three seconds later the center leaped above Eddie and tipped a missed shot into the basket—42–33.

Floyd called time-out.

"Calm down," he told the players at the bench. "We've got a long way to go." The players standing around him seemed stunned. Eddie's frustrations showed on his face. Eddie was not used to failure. Jimmy's miscue, Roy's bad pass, Gene's missed shot— these were not the stuff of the Falcons' basketball record.

"Hear me now," Floyd said. "We've got one change, just one, to make. With the Grizzlies keeping their forwards in close to help the center, we're going to have more openings than ever before from the outside. Pick those openings and shoot. Forget about Eddie under the basket unless he gets there alone by beating them down the court or until they have to pull those forwards back out."

The players were staring blankly at Floyd.

"And forget those errors. Everybody makes errors." He looked at Jimmy. "I stepped out of bounds once myself," he said. Jimmy did not smile. Floyd looked at Roy. "Long passes get intercepted sometimes," he said. "It's a fact of life." Roy nodded. "It is defense that will beat the Grizzlies, so press them—press them hard—and make your own breaks. We can come back. Nine points is not impossible. Not the way we like to run 'em."

He sent the players back onto the court, this time with William in the lineup. William replaced Ray, with Gene moving into the guard position and William at forward. Not only was a rest period useful for Ray, but Floyd figured William's height might help.

As he sat down on the bench next to Ray, Floyd thought, No, nine points is not impossible, but it's pretty close to it.

The clock showed three minutes of the third quarter gone.

Roy, standing out of bounds under the basket to throw the ball in, looked far downcourt. For a frightening moment Floyd thought he was going to uncork a long pass. The setting was wrong. The Grizzlies already were dropping back deep. A long pass was too risky. One more turnover, and one more Grizzlies' field goal, was sure to flatten the Falcons. But Roy turned and tossed the ball to Gene. Gene dribbled methodically toward the center stripe.

The Grizzlies' tall threesome was moving around in the lane in front of the basket. Eddie was trying to stay in front of them.

At the center stripe Gene passed across the court to Roy. Roy shot a pass to Jimmy, heading for the corner. Jimmy took in the pass, dribbled once, and went up. His jump shot easily cleared the outstretched hands of the shorter of the Grizzlies' forwards moving out toward him. The ball dropped—*swish!*—through the nets.

Floyd stood up, then sat back down. He took a deep breath. He could not remember a single field goal in the entire season that the Falcons needed more than that one. The drought was broken; the Grizzlies' run of points had been interrupted. The game was again within reasonable reach.

Then in the full-court press William boxed in a guard and forced a bad pass. Gene was there to scoop it up. He wriggled through a crowd of Grizzlies and tossed a one-hander toward the basket. The ball dropped through.

Floyd shot a glance at the scoreboard: Falcons 37, Grizzlies 42.

The Grizzlies struck back quickly. A long pass over the full-court press had just enough height and distance to carry beyond William's outstretched hands. The Grizzlies' shorter forward took in the pass. Alone and six feet in front of the racing William, he dribbled in, went up, and laid the ball in the basket.

The pattern seemed set again. The two teams were back to swapping field goals, the Grizzlies cashing in on their height under the basket, the Falcons making their own breaks with the full-court press and the pell-mell attack. It was a replay of the first half. But this time the Falcons were dangerously far behind—seven points, nine points, seven points again, five points, then back to seven points—as the final seconds of the third quarter ran off the clock.

The scoreboard at the buzzer showed: Falcons 45, Grizzlies 54.

Floyd faced six, not five, winded and perspiring players at the bench. William had played almost the entire third quarter, first spelling Ray, then Roy, then Gene. Eddie and Jimmy had stayed in all the way and were sure now to stay in to the finish.

"Okay?" Floyd asked Eddie.

"I'm okay," Eddie said. He sounded like he meant it.

"You?" Floyd asked Jimmy.

"Uh-huh," Jimmy puffed.

"The full-court press is going to win this game," Floyd said. He looked at the twins. They were the point men of the full-court press. They had taken the most minutes of rest on the bench in the third quarter, and now they had to be ready. "We've got to get the ball time and again and quickly, and we've got to shoot fast. The clock is against us. Don't let the Grizzlies dribble around. Don't let them toss passes back and forth. The clock will be ticking all the time. Take the ball away from them and shoot. Okay?"

The heads around him nodded.

"Watch their forwards," he continued. "They'll be giving us our signals. If they move out, send the ball in to Eddie. He will beat their center. But if they stay in, forget about him. He's outnumbered. And you'll be free to shoot from the outside."

Floyd sent the original starting five back onto the court. He glanced at the clock and the scoreboard— eight minutes to make up nine points.

In short order, a tip-in by Eddie and a driving lay-up by Roy cut the Grizzlies' lead to five, 54–49, before the Grizzlies scored on a baseline shot by the taller of the forwards.

Five and a half minutes remained on the clock.

Floyd was on his feet. The noise of the crowd was deafening, practically blotting out even his thoughts. The glare of the playing court seemed more brilliant than ever, almost blinding.

The Grizzlies trapped Gene at the sideline and took the ball away. With a quick pass to their center under the basket, they had another two points. The difference stood at nine again, 58–49.

Floyd felt himself sag. His own halftime prophecy was coming true. The first minutes of the second half were a dangerous time. A team made a run of points, took a decisive lead, and held on for victory. The Grizzlies' eight-point run loomed larger with every tick of the clock.

The Falcons came running back with three quick passes, Roy inbounds to Ray, Ray across the court to Jimmy, Jimmy to the inside to Eddie, who had beaten everyone to the lane. Eddie laid it in.

A seven-point difference, 58–51.

The full-court press paid the ultimate dividend for the first time. The Grizzlies' guard, standing out of bounds, was unable to find an opening in the tight line of Falcons chasing his teammates. Time ran out on the ten-second limit for the throw-in, and the Falcons got the ball out of bounds.

Ray sent a bounce pass to Jimmy. Jimmy fired and hit. A five-point difference, 58–53, with just over three minutes remaining.,

Nobody in the arena was seated. Floyd and his three substitutes stood at the sideline. Across the scorer's table, Marsh Carrington, his assistants, and his players were also standing. All around the arena, people were on their feet, roaring their cheers.

Again, the Falcons' full-court press went to work.

This time the guard did not let the clock defeat him. He got his pass off. Jimmy got a hand on the ball, but it wasn't enough. The shorter Grizzlies' forward batted the ball away and raced toward it to pick up the dribble. But the ball wasn't there when he arrived. Eddie had it. He fired from the edge of the keyhole. The ball hit the side of the rim and dropped into Jimmy's hands. The taller forward swarmed over him. Jimmy got a bounce pass off to Roy. Roy, coming in, was alone under the basket. He laid it in.

A three-point difference, 58–55, with two and a half minutes remaining.

Marsh Carrington called time-out.

The Grizzlies' guard stood out of bounds with the ball, trying to find a hole in the line of Falcons weaving around in front of him. The big center backed off from the crowd. Eddie went with him, but a step behind. The guard sent a high pass sailing to the center. Eddie leaped, an arm extended. Coming down, his shoulder bumped the center's arm. The ball rolled free. Jimmy chased the loose ball, but the referee's whistle stopped the play.

Eddie, his head lowered, lifted his hand, acknowledging the foul. It was his fourth. One more and he went to the bench.

At the sideline, Floyd clapped his hands together and shouted, "Okay, okay," with an enthusiasm he did not feel. He did not want Eddie or Jimmy or any of them in foul trouble at the end. And also, the Grizzlies were good free-throw shooters. They would like nothing better than to spend the last two minutes of the game plunking in free throws.

The center stepped to the free-throw line and tossed in the first of a one-and-one. Then he dropped in the bonus shot.

The Grizzlies went back to a five-point lead, 60–55. The clock showed just over two minutes remaining.

Roy tossed the ball inbounds to Ray. Ray shot a long pass across the court to Jimmy at the center stripe. He dribbled down the sideline. The Grizzlies' forwards hung back with the center. Jimmy turned, jumped, and shot. The ball smacked into the backboard and went in and then out and fell into Gene's hands. Gene got a shot off before the tall threesome could reach him. The shot scored.

Three points, 60–57. Just under two minutes remaining.

The Grizzlies' guard fired a pass just beyond Gene's reach to get the ball inbounds. The shorter forward grabbed the ball. He turned and dribbled down the sideline, crossing the center stripe. His teammates raced past him, taking up their attack positions. For almost a full minute they dribbled and passed the ball around the perimeter, eluding the frantic stabs of Jimmy, Gene, and the twins.

Then, with a carelessness Floyd could not believe, a guard standing with the ball back near the center stripe turned and flipped a pass toward his partner at guard.

Roy took off like a bullet coming out of the barrel of a rifle. Both hands in front of him, he leaped into the ball's path. One of his hands hit it. The ball bounded down the court. Roy lunged after it. He caught up with the ball just inside the free-throw line. He was alone. He dribbled once and twirled the ball upward. It rolled across the backboard and dropped through.

One point, 60–59. Fifty-two seconds remaining.

Twenty-one

Jimmy, first to arrive, grabbed Roy in a bear hug and swung him around. Leaping and holding a clenched fist high, Gene ran up to them and clapped Roy on the back.

"Get set! Get set!" Floyd shouted from the sideline. He feared that the Grizzlies, moving quickly, were going to pass inbounds before the Falcons got their full-court press in position. His voice was lost in the roar of the crowd.

Eddie ran into the scene and started shouting and pulling players into position.

The referee handed the ball to the Grizzlies' guard out of bounds under the basket. In front of the guard, the Falcons were in place and ready.

The loud cheers of the crowd turned into a chant. *"Get that ball! Get that ball! Fal-cons! Fal-cons! Get that ball!"* Floyd felt the throbbing beat of the chant in his breastbone.

The Grizzlies' guard looked at the nine players darting around in front of him. He waited. Then the shorter of the forwards started in one direction, reversed himself, and cut in front of Gene. The guard zipped the ball to him.

Gene, with Ray, swarmed over the forward. He pivoted, holding the ball away from them. Ray moved around toward the ball. The forward sent a bounce pass under Ray's arm. The taller of the forwards was there to get it. He turned and dribbled over the center stripe.

The Grizzlies had escaped.

Forty-one seconds remaining.

The Grizzlies' guards took turns dribbling crazily along the center stripe. Then one of them passed down the sideline to a forward. Gene moved in on him. The forward dribbled carefully. For a moment Floyd thought he was going to take a shot, but he didn't. He turned and sent the ball back out to one of the guards.

Thirty seconds remaining.

The roar of the crowd rolled down onto the court from all sides. Floyd did not hear it. He heard nothing. The fans—all sixteen thousand of them—were on their feet. Floyd did not see them. He stood at the sideline, hands stuffed in hip pockets, staring at the action near midcourt.

The months of practice, all the games, all the good plays and the bad, the happy and the troublesome moments—it all came down to this, to the last half minute of the season, with a championship in the balance.

One more theft of the ball. Then one more field goal. Just one. That was all that was needed.

Floyd weighed the merits of signaling the twins to foul. Sending the Grizzlies to the free-throw line was one way to stop the stall. But he did not want to do it. The Grizzlies were good free-throw shooters. The odds favored them scoring instead of missing and leaving the ball up there for grabs. Beyond that, even if the shooter missed, all of that height up there on the backboard gave the Grizzlies the advantage in going after the rebound. The odds favored them regaining possession of the ball or, worse yet, tipping it in for a field goal. No, Floyd did not want to signal the twins to foul. Not yet. But time was running out. He might have to take the gamble. It might be the Falcons' only chance.

Fifteen seconds remaining.

Floyd stepped forward. He waved a hand, trying to catch the eye of one of his players, any of them. They had to foul now. Maybe he had already waited too long.

The Grizzlies guard was dribbling toward the sideline. Roy was with him. Gene lunged forward and got between the dribbler and his partner at guard. The move left the forward free down the sideline, but Roy, guarding the dribbler, was blocking that avenue. The guard stopped dribbling. He had no escape valve. Roy pressed in close and reached for the ball.

193

The guard pivoted. With his back to Roy, he tried to pass down the sideline to the forward. Roy got a hand on the ball. For what seemed like a full minute, the ball hung in the air, going nowhere. The Grizzlies' guard reached for it. Roy reached for it. They both seemed to be moving in slow motion.

Roy had it. He turned, holding the ball in both hands.

Gene's voice, a scream, rang out above the cheers of the crowd. *"Time!"*

Nine seconds remaining.

Floyd told his players at the bench, "Get the ball to Jimmy in the corner."

Jimmy nodded. He had to do it one more time, the fall-away jump shot from the corner.

Floyd turned to Roy. "You take the ball out of bounds. Make them think that your pass is going to Ray. But get the ball to Gene. Okay?"

Gene was the best passer on the team and the steadiest floor player. He offered the best chance of finding a way to get the ball to Jimmy in the corner.

Roy nodded.

Floyd looked at Gene.

"Uh-huh," Gene said.

The teams lined up for the inbounds pass.

Ray and Gene moved out in the same direction. Roy watched Ray. Gene cut in front of Ray. Roy kept his eyes on Ray. He shot a bullet pass to Gene. Gene caught the ball and dribbled along the sideline. Jimmy drifted toward the basket, looking back at

Gene. The Grizzlies' taller forward moved with Jimmy. Jimmy cut sharply and darted around the forward, heading for the corner. Gene sent the ball into the empty space in front of Jimmy. Jimmy caught the ball and turned.

Four seconds remaining.

"Shoot," Floyd murmured to himself.

Jimmy eyed the basket. He started up. The forward was turning into Jimmy's line of sight.

Two seconds remaining.

Jimmy fired. The shot cleared the tall forward's upraised hands. The ball arched high.

The arena was deathly silent.

The ball came down. It hit the rim. It bounced away. It fell to the floor.

The buzzer sounded, ending the game.

A cheer erupted from the Fort Garrison fans behind Floyd. A loud *Oooooh* swept around the rest of the arena.

Floyd stood unmoving for a second. The leaping players in the royal-blue uniforms with white trim were a blur. The Fort Garrison fans now surging around Floyd and heading for their team on the court were a blur. He saw one thing clearly: Jimmy, across the court, in the corner, his arms hanging limply at his sides, his head bowed, tears streaming down his face. Eddie appeared. He embraced Jimmy. One of the twins arrived and put an arm around Jimmy's waist. The twin's number was hidden in the crowd so Floyd did not know who it was. Was it the one who had snapped at Jimmy? The swarming crowd blocked them all from view.

Floyd plunged into the crowd, heading for Jimmy. He met them all together at midcourt.

Floyd put his arms around Jimmy. "You played a great game," he said.

Then with his arm around Jimmy's shoulder, Floyd led his players in a weaving path through the crowd to the dressing room.

The dressing room was quiet.

No one was heading for the showers. The players, still in their uniforms, slumped on benches, some leaning back against the lockers, others leaning forward with elbows on knees, staring at the floor. The five starters were wet with perspiration and still breathing heavily.

Floyd took a seat on a bench next to Eddie and the twins, facing Jimmy and Gene on the bench across from him.

"I'm very proud of all of you," he said softly. "You should be very proud of yourselves."

Jimmy was looking at Floyd. The tears were gone, but he was wearing the unhappiest face Floyd had ever seen.

Floyd managed a grin. "You're going to be dreaming about that shot for a long, long time," he said. "But you must always remember all the other shots. You played a brilliant game." He paused. "And you know, we would not have been playing here tonight, not playing here at all, if it had not been for you."

Jimmy clenched his fists. The tears started again. "They got the ball to me," he said, "and I missed."

There was a knock at the door.

"Leave it alone," Floyd said. "They can wait."

He turned back to Jimmy. "You played one of the greatest games I've ever seen out there tonight," he said. "Don't ever forget that."

Jimmy nodded.

"You all, all of you, were great. Don't ever forget that."

The knocking at the door resumed.

"I'll see who it is," Floyd said, getting to his feet.

He opened the door a couple of inches and saw Gene's father. "Oh, c'mon in," Floyd said, starting to open the door.

"Wait a minute," Wilson Montomery said. He lowered his voice to a whisper and spoke.

Floyd raised an eyebrow in surprise as he listened. Then he glanced back at his players. He opened the door. "Okay, sure," he said.

Gene's father led a procession of Cedar Grove people into the dressing room, each carrying a bulky gray cardboard box.

"Your letter jackets are here," Floyd said.

Last through the door was John Raymond. Beyond him, Floyd saw the corridor filled with familiar faces from Cedar Grove, faces he had known all his life. The people were quiet and their expressions were somber. Floyd left the dressing-room door open.

The players opened boxes and removed the jackets, red with black trim, each with a huge CG on the left breast.

Big John was smiling.

"He made me promise not to tell you before the game," Gene's father said.

"We had a heck of a time tracking these things down, the right colors and all, on such short notice," Big John said. "Had to drive to Little Rock for them."

Floyd's eyes met Big John's and Floyd nodded his thanks.

"I want to make a very short speech," Big John said. He waited until he had everyone's attention. "We're all mighty proud of you," he said. "That's all, just mighty proud."

Somebody near the door started applauding. The noise spread through the crowd of people jammed into the dressing room and in the corridor outside.

Floyd waited a moment and then raised his hands for quiet. "I want to make a short speech, too." he said. "We showed 'em who the Falcons are. They know we'll be back next year. And we *will* be back next year." He looked at his younger brother. "Eddie will have to watch from the stands with you folks. But we'll have William under the basket, and we'll be back—all the rest of us—and we'll show 'em again who we are."

Floyd looked at Gene. He remembered the boy's shocked expression in the doorway of the office only hours earlier. Gene managed a small smile and nodded slightly.

Gene's father clapped Floyd on the shoulder and said, "That's good news."

"And next year," Big John said, "we'll have to do something about those uniforms."

"What?" Jimmy said. "There's nothing wrong with these uniforms."

Even the twins smiled.

ABOUT THE AUTHOR

Thomas J. Dygard has been praised by *Booklist* as being "consistently one of the ablest writers of teenage sports fiction." He began his career as a sportswriter for the *Arkansas Gazette* in Little Rock and joined the Associated Press in 1954. In the years that followed, he worked in AP offices in Little Rock, Detroit, Birmingham, New Orleans, Indianapolis, Chicago, and Tokyo.

His popular books for young readers include *Halfback Tough, Outside Shooter, Quarterback Walk-on,* and *Tournament Upstart*.